SEEKER

SIGNS OF THE PROPHECY BOOK TWO

DEBBIE MUMFORD

WDM
Publishing

The Saga Continues...

Lilith, the self-styled Queen of Darkness— an *Old One* who rebelled against High Magic— was determined to kill Gwen Vaughan. The sorceress had made her first attempt when Gwen was a child, long before Gwen had awakened to who, and what, she really was.

Gwen had survived, thanks to the quick action of her *Old One* guardian, Dylan Kincaid... but her parents had not. To protect her, Dylan had been forced to remove her from everything and everyone she'd ever known. He'd placed her on a ranch in Colorado, with friends from her parents' college days. Good people, but ones who had lost touch with the Vaughans simply because their lives had taken them in different directions.

Dylan had done his work well. Gwen remained hidden until her power blossomed. But when she came into her own, Lilith began to hunt her again.

Fortunately, Gwen could fend for herself now... especially when forewarned.

SIGNS OF THE PROPHECY SERIES:

Youngest
Seeker
Chosen

COPYRIGHT

Praise for *Her Highland Laird*:

Katharina from Amazon: Five stars: "I'm normally not someone who reads romance novels, but … I stumbled over Debbie Mumford's Romance stories. This one was an absolute treat. Not only did it depict the life in 15th century correctly (well researched for such a short story), it evokes emotion very well … I'll definitely read more by this author."

~

Tony from Amazon: Five stars: "Very interesting story. With some suspense and an interesting thread of love."

~

Praise for *Second Sight*:

Bookgirl from Amazon: Five stars: "A lost love, a new love, psychic magic, a murder and a tiger! Wow. I loved this book. It was fast paced and easy to read. I got caught up in the "I'll just read one more chapter" syndrome and lost a bit of sleep but it was worth it. I hope Ms. Mumford writes more in this world. I love these characters."

~

Dragon Slayer from Amazon: Five stars: "I liked the characters and the story line. For those that love a mystery and a good romance along with the paranormal, this book is for you."

For everyone who's ever dreamed that magic was real...

PROLOGUE

*H*igh Magic called, and the Youngest obeyed.

High Magic created and power awoke
An Old One stands ready to take up her yoke.
A new millennium reigns, and science is crowned.
The Balance has shifted and evil abounds.

At solstice and equinox and four fire feasts,
With vision and power, the Old One seeks
A sigil of balance by seven signs made,
'Twill be the undoing of the Dark now arrayed.

Guinevere Enid Vaughan's quest as High Magic's Seeker was underway; three signs already dangled from the silver bracelet encircling her wrist. Four more would be required before her task was complete.

CHAPTER 1

Gwen Vaughan and Rachel Carson, recently reunited childhood best friends, strolled casually down the street near Gwen's Portland, Oregon apartment. It was the Fourth of July, and the two young women had decided to celebrate their freedom with a trip to the Portland Art Museum. Since it was a beautiful summer day and the museum was only a few blocks from Gwen's apartment, they had decided to walk.

"I've always loved these park blocks between the Portland State and the museum," Rachel said as they ambled along enjoying the sunlight filtering through the green of the park's trees. "I'm so glad you chose that apartment. Now I've got an excuse to loiter in the park."

Gwen laughed. "Happy to be of service," she said with a mock bow.

"Here it is." Rachel indicated the massive building across the street from where they stood. Heading to the corner, the young women crossed the street and ascended the broad steps leading up to the main entrance.

As they stood in line to buy their tickets, Gwen noted the combination of cool marble stairs and warm wood parquet floors with approval. *Balance,* she thought, *this place is in balance. No wonder it radiates such a soothing atmosphere for its patrons.*

The concept of balance was more important to Gwen now than it had been a few months earlier... before she'd learned her true identity.

Back in December, on her twenty-second birthday, she'd discovered that the world wasn't what she'd always assumed. That *she* wasn't who she thought she was. Through a totally unexpected and altogether disquieting vision, she'd learned that she, Guinevere Enid Vaughan, wasn't even human; she was the youngest *Old One.* A member of a virtually immortal race. Born to perfectly normal, human parents, but called by High Magic to a life of service to the Light.

Since her awakening, Gwen had dedicated herself to maintaining the balance between Light and Dark, to defending the mortal world she was no longer a part of. But whether she was human or an immortal *Old One*, Gwen still enjoyed spending time with her friends, and today that included a trip to the museum.

Gwen and Rachel spent several hours contemplating the various styles of art showcased by the large museum. When their protesting feet and legs finally convinced them they couldn't handle another moment of standing in awed appreciation, they strolled to the elegant little café and collapsed into comfortable chairs.

"I didn't realize you were so taken with Asian art," Gwen said after ordering a summer salad with shrimp and an iced tea.

"Oh, yes," Rachel breathed, "this whole area is permeated with a strong Asian influence. I'm not sure how you could grow up here and not respond to it. We'll have to visit the Chinese Garden and the Japanese Garden soon. They're so beautiful."

While her friend rhapsodized about the wonders of the art and architecture of the Far East, Gwen gradually became aware of an intensity of interest that seemed to be centered on herself and Rachel. Her pulse quickened as this unexpected scrutiny claimed her full attention. Quickly, she scanned the room. The café was nearly empty, a fact that had allowed her to notice the observation. She allowed her senses to roam across the little gift shop that sat just beyond the opening to the café...

...and found her quarry. A good-looking young man, dark-haired, and not much older than she and Rachel, watched their table with single-minded interest.

She glanced quickly back to Rachel in order to avoid making eye contact with the man. No need to alert him to the fact that she'd noticed his attention. Making a few affirmative noises for Rachel's benefit, she allowed the surface of her mind to rest lightly on their conversation, while the main part of her awareness remained on the unknown man observing them.

She searched her memory; she was certain she had seen his face before.

Of course. He had been rearranging a display in the Asian Art exhibit. Fine, he was a museum employee. Was he wearing an identification badge?

Gwen chanced a quick glance in his direction, and confirmed that he did indeed have a badge clipped to his suit jacket.

Had they done something wrong? Something to suggest they might be art thieves? A chill stole across her soul, and she worked to suppress a shiver of fear as her mind leapt to the next logical conclusion.

Was he under the influence of Gwen's nemesis, Lilith?

For some reason no one was certain of, Lilith, the self-styled Queen of Darkness— an *Old One* who rebelled against High Magic— was determined to kill Gwen. The sorceress had made her first attempt when Gwen was a child, long before Gwen had awakened to who, and what, she really was.

Gwen had survived, thanks to the quick action of her *Old One* guardian, Dylan Kincaid... but her parents had not. To protect her, Dylan had been forced to remove her from everything and everyone she'd ever known. He'd placed her on a ranch in Colorado, with friends from her parents' college days. Good people, but ones who had lost touch with the Vaughans simply because their lives had taken them in different directions.

Dylan had done his work well. Gwen remained hidden until her power bloomed. But when she came into her own, Lilith began to hunt her again.

Fortunately, now Gwen could fend for herself... especially when forewarned.

She raised her eyes again and studied the young man's face, her mind running through the sigils that would be most effective in disabling him in such a public place.

Ah-ha, no need. False alarm.

She smiled to herself, allowing her defenses to return to their normal state. The man wasn't interested in Gwen at all. His attention was clearly fixed on Rachel. When she studied him that last time, her concern banished by decision, she'd been able to observe him in more detail. He was clearly focused on the lovely blonde woman sitting across the table from her.

No longer feeling threatened, Gwen realized she had been stealing glances at him through an exceptionally clear aura. No malice muddied her perceptions of his face and form. The man wasn't a threat, but he was very interested in Rachel.

DAVID MOVED QUIETLY across the gift shop to get a better view of the two young women in the café. If he was honest with himself, which he always tried to be, he'd have to admit he was only interested in observing the diminutive blonde. He watched in delight as she tossed her head and laughed animatedly, her honey blonde curls shining in the clear sunlight streaming through the large café windows. He hadn't been close enough yet to determine her eye color, but it didn't matter. They were large and intelligent, and sparkled with mischief as she chatted happily with her dark-haired friend.

The young women stood, preparing to leave.

He panicked.

He had to meet her. He couldn't just let her walk out of the museum, he might never find her again. What could he say? How could he approach her? He watched as they paid for their lunch, thoughts running furiously through his mind.

They walked toward him. In a moment they would be past him—on their way into the huge city that waited outside the museum's doors. This was it. It was now or never.

GWEN WATCHED the young man surreptitiously as she and Rachel made their way to the front of the gift shop and the high-ceilinged museum entrance. She could almost see the panic racing across his expressive face. She hid a smile behind a counterfeit cough as they drew even with him. As she had expected, he stepped into their path, blocking their progress.

Rachel stopped and glanced up at him, startled by his sudden appearance.

"Excuse me, ladies." His voice sounded slightly strangled, but he cleared his throat and continued. "I couldn't help noticing your interest in the Asian Art exhibit. I wondered if you might like a tour of our acquisitions department?"

Oh, please! Gwen stifled the desire to roll her eyes. *That's got to be the worst pick-up line I've ever heard.*

Rachel frowned at the earnest young man. "A tour of the acquisitions department? Are you for real?"

The young man flushed to the roots of his dark brown hair. "My name is David Milligan," he said, moving a hand to indicate his name badge. "I'm the assistant to the curator for the Asian Art department. If you're interested, I'd be happy to show you around our acquisitions department." As he spoke he escorted them out of the gift shop and into the spacious entrance hall.

"Nice to meet you, David Milligan." Gwen's comment forced the young man to turn his attention to her... and look away from Rachel. "I'm Guinevere Vaughan and this is Rachel Carson. We'd love a behind-the-scenes tour," she smiled as his face lit with relief, "but not today. Shall we call your office for an appointment?"

The smile froze on his face, but he recovered his poise and reached into his jacket pocket. Pulling out a business card, he handed it to Gwen.

"That would be fine. Please ask for me by name. Good afternoon, Miss Vaughan, Miss Carson." His gaze lingered on Rachel's face for a moment, then he turned and walked away.

Rachel followed his progress until he turned a corner, then she sighed and looked at Gwen. "Was that what I think it was?" she asked with a nervous giggle.

Gwen shushed her. "We'll talk when we get outside."

They hurried out the door, down the wide steps and across the street into the park. Once there, Gwen's control broke and she chanted in the sing-song pattern of a ten-year-old, "Rachel's got a boyfriend!"

Rachel promptly responded by hitting her. "And how do you know it's me he was after? You're the one holding his card." But she blushed, looking very pleased.

"Yeah, right, he was so interested in me that he could hardly tear his eyes away from you," Gwen teased, grinning broadly. She handed Rachel his card. "So, are you going to call and make an appointment?"

"Definitely!" she said, her eyes widening as she grasped Gwen's hands. "You'll come with me, won't you?" The pleading note in her voice was unmistakable. "I mean, why did you say we'd make an appointment, anyway?"

"Of course I'll come with you. I wouldn't miss the sequel to this encounter for the world." She expertly dodged the purse Rachel swung at her before continuing. "I said we'd make an appointment so the ball would be in your court. I figured you deserved the chance to decide whether you wanted to follow through without him looming over you."

Rachel's eyes glazed, her expression bemused. "He did kind of tower over me, didn't he? What would you guess? Six foot... maybe six-two?"

"Well, anyone looks tall to you, midget," Gwen chortled.

"I am not a midget. I'm five-two. And very happy with my height, thank you very much." She tried to look annoyed, but failed miserably. The friends lapsed into silence as Rachel stared dreamily into space.

CHAPTER 2

A week later David Milligan waited with nervous anticipation for Rachel—and Gwen—to arrive at the Museum's administrative offices. He didn't want to appear too eager, but found he couldn't sit still. So, he compromised by pacing up and down a hallway just out of sight of the entrance he'd suggested they use. He was at the far end of the hall when he heard the lilting music of their voices. He curbed his impulse to run and managed to approach them at what he hoped was a sedate walk.

"Good morning, ladies." He extended his arm to shake hands—first with Rachel, then Gwen. "I'm so glad you could make it." They walked to the security desk and picked up a temporary name tag for each young woman. "Please follow me."

Gwen drifted along behind David and Rachel, barely listening as they talked about Asian art, architecture, color theory, interior design, and the merits of Feng Shui in American homes and offices. Well aware that she was along merely as a chaperone on this particular outing, Gwen did her best to remain quiet and unobtrusive.

I'm not sure I'm cut out to be a duenna. She smiled, envisioning herself as a Spanish matron wrapped in yards of black lace. But she doubted she'd be called into service for these two again. They seemed to be hitting it off nicely, and they definitely had a lot in common.

The trio spent the better part of an hour touring the facility and Gwen found herself fascinated by the processes involved in examining and cataloguing the many pieces of art that came into the museum, whether they were to be permanent additions or temporary displays. She had the opportunity to closely observe a carved funerary urn and was pleased to see that its inscription was intact. David noticed her interest and launched into a detailed description.

"I hate to contradict you, David," Gwen interrupted, "but you've got your facts confused."

 David stopped and blinked. "Excuse me? Why would you say that?"

Gwen hesitated a moment then pointed to the incised lettering. "The inscription clearly states that this urn contains the remains of a child, not a warrior."

"You can read the inscription?" His voice registered shock and disbelief. "Didn't you say you were a student?"

"Well, yes. I'm a graduate student at PSU... in Linguistic Anthropology. I already hold a BA in Linguistics. Ancient languages are my specialty." Gwen smiled at his look of surprised respect.

"I don't suppose you'd be interested in a part-time job, would you?"

"A job?" Now it was Gwen's turn to express surprise. A job had been the furthest thing from her mind, but she was going to need one eventually.

David hurried on, using her surprised silence to state his case. "Of course, I can't promise anything, but I can get you an interview with the curator. I know he's been looking for someone to do translation when the need arises. If you're interested, we can head back to my office and I'll see what I can arrange."

Gwen nodded, exchanged a bewildered look with Rachel, and trailed along in David's wake. When they arrived at the office area, David wasted no time. He fired staccato questions at the secretarial staff who answered with equal rapidity and an amazing conservation of words. Then he herded the young women through a maze of corridors, coming to rest at last inside a spacious conference room.

"David, wait a minute." Gwen was dazed by the concept of an impromptu job interview. "I'm not prepared for this. I don't have a resume; I'm not dressed for an interview... and I haven't got the foggiest notion what a linguist would do in a museum." Her agitation wasn't lessened by the silly grin that appeared on his face.

"Hey, turn-about's fair play." David crowed with delight. "You turned the tables on me the other day. Now I get to return the favor." He laughed at her look of consternation and gestured for her to take a seat. "Don't worry, Gwen. Eric knows you're not prepared for this. Just tell him what you know. We can get a resume and transcript later... if they're needed."

Collapsing into a chair, Gwen narrowed her eyes and studied David in exasperation, but detected no muddying of his aura. Evidently this was just what it seemed, a spur of the moment opportunity, with no malice intended. Actually, David appeared to be quite excited at having found a qualified candidate for his superior to interview.

Glancing at Rachel who sat at ease in one of the conference chairs, intently watching David's every move, Gwen relaxed. She hadn't been looking for a job, so she had nothing at stake, and this bizarre twist was giving Rachel a totally different view of David's character. Since the young man was no longer completely absorbed in making a good impression, Rachel was being allowed a peek into his unguarded nature.

The worst that could happen was that Gwen would make a fool of herself. An ironic little smile lifted the corners of her mouth. Her pride could handle the potential hit if it helped Rachel make an informed decision about this young man.

David turned as a middle-aged man strode into the room. Tall and thin with salt and pepper hair, he glanced quickly around the room, taking in all the details of the tableau before him. He stepped to Gwen with assurance and offered his hand.

"Miss Vaughan, I'm Eric Lundrigan. I'm pleased to meet you." He gave Gwen a confident smile, then turned to David. "David, why don't you and Miss... " he consulted a card in his hand "Carson wait in the foyer. We'll join you in a few moments."

Rachel rose gracefully, squeezed Gwen's shoulder as she passed, and, without a word, walked through the door David held open. The young man followed her out, closing the door behind himself.

Gwen turned to face Eric Lundrigan. "Thank you for seeing me on such short notice, sir," she began, "I'm afraid I'm not at all prepared for this. I didn't come expecting an interview, especially for employment."

Eric smiled. "Please sit, Gwen. May I call you Gwen?"

"Certainly, sir."

"Then, please, drop the 'sir' and call me Eric." His eyes twinkled with amusement, and Gwen relaxed, feeling more comfortable with the whole situation. "David tells me that you're a linguist. Please, tell me about your training."

After giving him a quick verbal version of her resume, Gwen paused to ask a question of her own. "What kind of work do you have in mind? David was very sketchy on details."

"Actually, I think this might suit you perfectly. We've had trouble filling the position because all the qualified candidates were looking for full-time employment. We need someone who can check the translations on artifacts which come in bearing language components. Most often these will be short translations, similar to the funerary urn which landed you in this room." He paused, smiling as she blushed at the memory. "However, there will be the occasional manuscript or more complex tablet. Also, we sometimes receive traveling displays from museums in other countries. When that happens we need our own translations of the contracts, as well as translations of the information cards to be used in the exhibit."

Gwen nodded. "So, would you need me on a regular basis, or would you prefer me to be an on-call consultant?"

"Both, actually," he replied. "I think we could guarantee you about ten hours a week of regular employment, though some of that time might be spent doing cataloguing if nothing needed translation."

"That would be fine," Gwen said, "I would enjoy working with the artifacts, and cataloguing is a very familiar task."

"Then there will be occasional periods when we will need your assistance nearly full-time. I realize you have other obligations. We'll make every effort not to overtax you when those rare events occur."

"That sounds like a reasonable approach."

"Now, let's get down to compensation." Eric rubbed his palms together in anticipation of a completed transaction. They spent the next few minutes putting together a job description and compensation package for Gwen's new position.

~

DAVID POSITIVELY BEAMED when he saw Gwen and Eric approaching, chatting quietly. He'd done it. He'd found a part-time translator for Eric. Not only that, he had found the woman of his dreams.

It had been a very good morning for David Milligan.

"Congratulations, Gwen." David shook her hand enthusiastically after Eric excused himself to return to his office. "This calls for a celebration. How about lunch?" He grinned. The thought of spending more time with Rachel made him lightheaded and just a bit giddy. "My treat." he added quickly as he saw the friends exchange glances.

"Oh, David. I think you've caused quite enough trouble for one day." Gwen laughed as his mood plummeted. "Of course, we'll celebrate with lunch. But you're not buying, I am. After all, you just got me a great part-time job... one that even relates to my studies. I owe you one. Let's start the payment plan with lunch."

Relief washed over him. He didn't have to say good-bye to Rachel yet.

Then the best thing happened... the woman of his dreams took David's arm with a proprietary air and propelled him toward the door. "I know just the spot. We'll have you back to work in an hour or so." Rachel beamed up at him. "Of course, Mr. Lundrigan looked pleased enough that you could probably get away with anything today."

Laughing, the new friends walked out into the bright summer sunshine, each thinking that it was truly a glorious day to be alive.

CHAPTER 3

*D*avid Milligan had staked his claim on a place in Gwen's and Rachel's lives.

With Gwen, he earned the titles of "friend" and "colleague." Not only had he gotten her the job in the first place, but he proved to be a reliable source of information and assistance as she learned her way around her assigned tasks. She found his cheerful, self-confident nature a delight, and was pleased that he considered her a friend as well.

For Rachel, David's insertion into their lives was much more complicated. It was clear to Gwen that they were a perfect match for each other. His easy-going charm sparked an intensity in Rachel's nature that Gwen had never guessed existed, while her friend's incandescent beauty called forth a gallantry that made him want to protect the young woman at all costs.

But it wasn't just her physical loveliness that had him besotted. The soundness of her character and clarity of soul shone with particular brilliance when she was with him. She was his treasure, and anyone who saw them together for more than a few minutes knew it.

But their relationship was volatile.

The passion that bound them together— and convinced Gwen that theirs would be a lasting union— sometimes erupted in flaming arguments that left them both exhausted and frightened.

With a wisdom beyond her years, Gwen knew that, if they survived their courtship and consummated their union, nothing would ever tear them apart. The sexual tension that blazed between them— unrelieved at the moment— would transmute into an unbreakable bond once they fully committed to each other.

Gwen watched the rapidity of their relationship's growth and longed to have the time and leisure to explore a similar bond with a certain *Old One* she'd come to rely on for his steady strength: Lorenzo Santini.

Renzo.

One of her *Old One* mentors, Renzo was a good-looking man with dark hair and warm, chocolate-brown eyes. While not movie star handsome, his chiseled chin, high cheekbones, and long, straight nose gave him a rugged, undeniably masculine charm.

He was also the man she was on the verge of falling in love with... a more than six-hundred year old man. But despite the vast differences in their physical ages, Renzo was also the next youngest *Old One*.

Their species was very rare indeed.

While she was delighted for Rachel and David, she was also envious of their growing attachment. She wished fervently that

Renzo was nearby so that they could explore their own relationship. Assuming, of course, that Renzo was even interested in her in a romantic way.

She knew he was fond of her, but sometimes she wondered if her infatuation with him caused her to read more into his words and actions than was truly there. What if he simply thought of her as the youngest *Old One*, a child, and was fond of her... and protective of her... the way all sane adults are protective of their young: as the future and continuation of the race?

Sitting at her dressing table beside a window overlooking a city park filled with emerald green grass and blooms of all colors, Gwen closed her eyes and endured a pang of longing as real as any physical ailment. She missed Renzo. It had been well over a month since she'd seen him, and it would be at least another few days before she had any hope of seeing him again.

On August first, the festival of Lughnasadh, he'd put in an appearance to guard her during the next phase of the quest she'd been called to complete: to find seven elemental signs that, when joined together, would create a new and powerful sigil for use by the *Old Ones* in service to High Magic and the Light.

Unfortunately, she also knew he'd vanish again as soon as the next sign was safely attached to the bracelet on her wrist.

And tonight she was expected to accompany Rachel and David to the opening of a new club. She sighed. She didn't feel like dancing and partying. Not without Renzo.

Maybe *Old Ones* didn't fall in love. Maybe she'd outgrow this infatuation with Renzo. Maybe he was intentionally staying away from her... waiting for her to grow up and stop embarrassing him with her puppy love. After all, she hadn't seen any indication that other *Old Ones* were in pairs. Maybe love was another sacrifice she was expected to make on the altar of magical power.

Gwen knew she'd never have children— she couldn't say she'd accepted the fact that *Old Ones* didn't reproduce, but she did know it— was she now expected to give up her dream of having the kind of love that Rachel and David were developing before her very eyes?

She opened her eyes and examined her face in the mirror. *You're jealous*, she thought with pinpoint accuracy, *and it's not a pretty sight.*

Gwen needed to get a grip. Rachel was very excited about their night out, and Gwen had no business spoiling the evening for her friends.

Wrenching her mind away from her misery at being separated from Renzo, Gwen made a determined effort to lighten her mood. Her mind drifted to her course work, and she gave a mental sigh of exasperation.

Thinking about Whittier's latest peevishness was definitely not going to improve her spirits.

Gwen had worked hard to carve out a niche for herself on campus during this summer session, and had gotten to know several of her fellow graduate students as well as most of the faculty members in her major departments: linguistics and anthropology.

There was only one flaw in her summer studies... one of her anthropology professors seemed to have taken an instant, and intense, dislike to her. Dr. Jason Whittier appeared to be a perfectly nice, middle-aged man, well-versed in his subject, and patient in his interactions with students.

Except for Gwen.

He couldn't even look at her without glaring and often answered her questions with snide quips that made her feel like an idiot.

When she'd asked him privately what she'd done to offend him, he had accused her of fraud, of entering the program under false credentials.

His animosity mystified her.

Unfortunately, she didn't know any of the faculty well enough to discuss the problem. She had an advisor, of course, but Whittier's dislike seemed too personal to take to an academic advisor.

But she could discuss the problem with Dylan. The *Old One* who had guarded her as a child and mentored her as she learned her power was accustomed to campus politics. He would give her sound advice.

Settling her dilemma with Whittier aside, Gwen thought about the last translation she'd done for the museum instead. Smiling, she remembered Eric Lundrigan's pleasure at how quickly and competently she had dealt with the tricky inscription.

Feeling a bit happier, she loaded a favorite jazz playlist and searched her closet for the perfect outfit to complete her transformation from morose doctoral candidate to sexy young woman.

An hour later she waited just inside the front hallway of her building for David and Rachel to pick her up. The outfit she'd chosen— a flaming red halter top that stopped just short of her waist and a pair of low slung black leather pants— showed off just enough bare midriff to give off a sexy vibe without appearing lewd. Her dark brown hair swung loose just below her shoulders. Parted on the left, its only restraint was a single silver clip at her right temple. The only jewelry Gwen wore was the silver bracelet with its disparate signs.

Simple and elegant; Gwen's favorite style.

She waited only a moment before her cell phone rang announcing Rachel and David's impending arrival. Gwen stepped out to the sidewalk just in time to hop in the back seat as David pulled his late model silver Honda Accord briefly to the curb.

"Perfect timing," Rachel grinned. "This is going to be so much fun. I'm so glad you could join us, Gwen."

Smiling without reservation, Gwen teased, "I just hope David agrees. I bet he'd just as soon have you all to himself."

"Too true," he quipped, "but if I have to share her with an entire club full of people, then I'm delighted to have you along as well." He smiled at her in the rearview mirror.

"Oh, well said," she laughed, "I do believe you've missed your calling. Quick, Rachel, where can we sign him up as a diplomat?"

The evening was a great success, and Gwen certainly didn't lack for partners when she chose to dance. The music was great, her companions were the best a young woman could ask for, and the atmosphere of the club was upbeat. All three of them were having a fabulous time.

As it neared time to call it a night, Gwen excused herself to visit the ladies' room. Rachel automatically rose to accompany her. The path across the dance floor toward the restroom was packed with merry-makers, but the young women threaded their way through to the access hall, a narrow corridor that continued past the restrooms to a closed alley exit.

As she approached the ladies' room, Gwen's *Old One* senses alerted her to a disturbance just beyond the rear door. Rachel, still focused on the music from the dance floor hadn't picked up on the terrified squealing of a dog in pain. To Gwen, however, the cries of the wounded animal were all too clear, and there was no way she could pretend she hadn't heard.

"You go ahead, Rachel," she said quietly, "I'm going to get a breath of fresh air first."

Rachel glanced apprehensively at the shadowed back door, but, at Gwen's bright smile of reassurance, shrugged and continued into the restroom.

Gwen called defensive sigils to mind as she walked to the door. She wasn't sure what she'd find on the other side, but she was determined to blast whoever was harming a helpless animal. She'd deal with the consequences later... a mild memory charm would probably be required once the dog had been released from its torment and healed.

Her thoughts consumed with rescuing the dog, Gwen didn't take time to probe the alleyway for danger.

She didn't think to determine how many miscreants were involved.

It didn't occur to her to wonder why anyone would torment an animal right outside a popular nightclub.

She simply followed her instinct to succor the wounded and stepped through that door...

...into her own personal hell.

CHAPTER 4

*T*wo men huddled over the body of an emaciated brown mongrel. Gwen strode toward them, fingers forming a sigil to freeze them where they knelt.

Focused as she was, she didn't notice the other two men... the ones who stepped from the shadows on either side of the door she had just come through.

Without hesitation, they grabbed her hands, immobilizing her fingers by interlacing them with their own.

Startled by their sudden appearance, and their immobilization of her hands, Gwen didn't scream. She struggled desperately to free her hands— she needed them to draw the sigils that would release her magic.

But the men's hold was too strong. She was locked in their grip.

As she fought to free herself, the other two men abandoned the dog and ran to join their comrades. One of them stuffed a nasty brown handkerchief in her mouth before jerking his head toward a white panel van parked a few yards further down the alley.

"Quick, get her in the van before someone happens along," he growled.

"Shouldn't we take care of her hands, like the lady said, before we try to get her away?" asked the hoodlum holding her left hand.

Her hands? Gwen's mind raced, trying to sort through her confusion and panic. Why were they focused on her hands? What lady?

When the fourth man yanked a baseball bat from the back of the van, her panic solidified into terror.

She struggled maniacally to free herself as the thugs dragged her closer to the van. She fought the gag with her tongue, made as much noise as she could through the muffling fabric.

All to no avail.

Gwen could neither stop her progress toward the van nor wrench her hands free from her captors.

The men dragged her behind the van's shielding bulk and pushed her roughly to the pavement. She squirmed on her belly, the damp asphalt tearing at her bare midriff, but couldn't escape.

The men flattened her hands against the grimy alley floor.

Her eyes widened in terror as the burly man raised the baseball bat and swung it down…

…smashing her right hand.

Her world exploded, senses reeling against excruciating pain.

She fought the wave of nausea that pounded against the gag, fought the blackness that wavered at the edges of her vision, threatening to steal her consciousness.

She couldn't faint.

She'd die if she didn't get help.

But she couldn't think. Couldn't push past the pain.

The thugs hooted with laughter, enjoying her agony even more than they'd enjoyed that miserable dog's.

The dog. That poor animal had suffered just to bait their trap... and it had worked.

Gwen's universe dwindled to the screaming nerve endings in her shattered right hand. She fought to calm her mind. To think. Had almost succeeded, when...

...a crushing blow to her left hand engulfed her mind in a red haze of searing pain.

She had no identity.

No consciousness.

No lucid thought patterns.

Only terror and anguish remained...

...and a flickering awareness that she would die if she didn't regain control of her senses.

A ragged corner of her mind caught the awareness of mortal peril and launched itself in a desperate scream for protection, for surcease from pain.

She didn't direct that primal cry. There was no thought attached. It simply drove into the minds of those she loved with a force that sent them to their knees.

~

RACHEL COLLAPSED in the ladies room, her mind unable to deal with the searing pain that shot through her soul.

. . .

DAVID FELL from the barstool where he had been talking to an acquaintance during the young women's absence.

DYLAN WINCED in agony and grabbed his head, hoping he could keep it from exploding... but he recognized the source and his face paled as he recognized Gwen's peril.

MEI, Gwen's *Old One* sponsor, sat down with a thud and buried her head in her hands. Once the initial shock passed, she cast her mind in search of the origin of Gwen's wordless scream.

BUT RENZO...

...Renzo threw himself straight into the maelstrom of Gwen's pain and materialized beside her before the brunt of her psychic blow even registered.

The miscreants who had captured and brutalized Gwen were pushing her battered body into the back of a van, laughing and crudely detailing the perverted acts they intended to perform on her body.

They didn't care if she survived, would enjoy it more if she didn't. They knew there would be no consequences.

The lady wanted her dead.

They could fulfill their nastiest sexual fantasies without concern. They'd see how long she survived the orgy, then they'd degrade her lifeless body. This gig was a sexual predator's wet dream. Pain, torture, sex and money... a mouth-watering combination.

Unfortunately for them, Renzo arrived and the dream ended... violently.

The fully functional, enraged *Old One* waded through the vermin who had dared to harm one of his own. He threw the thugs aside with careless ease, quickly clearing a path between himself and his Gwen.

Where each miscreant landed, he stayed... unable to move any muscle not directly involved in the continuation of his life.

One man hung upside down, pinioned to the brick wall of the alley.

Two others lay in tortured positions on the pavement.

The final culprit hung suspended above Renzo's head, having not yet landed when the immobility spell took effect.

Gwen lay crumpled on the pavement behind the van. Renzo knelt beside her, afraid to touch her lest he cause more pain.

This was the tableau David saw as he rushed through the club's alley door.

"Get away from her," he roared at Renzo, not stopping to notice the impossible positions of the other four men in the alley.

Renzo whirled to face him, prepared to attack this new threat to his beloved.

"Renzo, no," Gwen whispered, her voice hoarse and ragged.

At that moment Dylan and Mei appeared in the alley. Both took in the scene at a glance. Mei rushed to Gwen's side.

Dylan stepped to Renzo, his gaze glued to David's face. "Do you know what happened here?" His voice was deadly quiet, quivering with intensity.

Renzo shook his head, watching David warily. "I was about to add this one to my collection when Gwen stopped me. Is she conscious, Mei?"

"No," the *Old One* answered in crisp, clear tones, "I'm taking her to the glade for healing. Join me when you finish here." She placed one hand delicately on Gwen's shoulder, signing the transport sigil with the other.

They vanished.

David gave a startled cry as his battered friend disappear.

"Who are you?" He glared at the men standing in front of him. "What have you done to Gwen? What's with these other guys?" He gestured at the unnatural positions of the other men in the alley.

Dylan cocked his head and glanced at Renzo. "Why don't I do the mop up, while you deal with this young man?"

Renzo nodded his agreement. Now that Gwen was safe and being cared for, he acknowledged his own fear... and his body's reaction to his undisciplined flight to her side.

Holding his emotions firmly in check, he crossed to David. "It's okay. We're the cavalry. I'm Renzo Santini, a very good friend of Gwen's. Who are you?"

David eyed him warily, but said, "David Milligan. Gwen came here tonight with me and my girlfriend, Rachel."

Renzo's eyes lit. "Rachel Carson? Great, I know her." His shoulders relaxed. "She can vouch for both of us."

"Okay, so you know Rachel. That still doesn't explain where you came from, or what I've seen in this alley. I want... no, I *need* to understand what's going on. Something happened to me in there." He shrugged his shoulders and inclined his head to indicate the dance club.

"I can't explain it, but whatever it was knocked me off my chair. I don't know how, but I knew something was wrong with Gwen. I came barreling out here to find her... and found this mess instead. What gives, and where's Gwen?" As he spoke, his voice rose in both volume and intensity until he trembled as he said her name.

Renzo laid a calming hand on his shoulder. "Let's step inside. Do you know where Rachel is? Is she all right?"

David's eyes widened. "I've no idea. The last I knew both of them were headed to the restroom." He turned and lunged toward the van. "If those creeps hurt her..."

Stepping in front of him, Renzo stopped David's rush toward the parked vehicle. "She's not in the van. I'd know. Let's step inside and find her. If you were knocked off your chair by Gwen's scream, Rachel might have been incapacitated. She's much closer to Gwen, both emotionally and in physical location." Renzo made these statements matter-of-factly as he steered David through the door and into the corridor.

Upon reaching the ladies room they recognized the disorganized milling of disconcerted people.

"Excuse me," Renzo said, shouldering past several patrons, "I'm a doctor. Does someone need assistance?"

Immediately, the crowd parted, and Renzo and David saw Rachel lying on the floor in front of a bank of sinks.

"Let me through, please," Renzo continued until they stood beside her unconscious form. Renzo knelt and went through the motions of checking pulse and pupil reaction, while surreptitiously forming a sigil with a hand that seemed to be fumbling for something in his jacket pocket.

Rachel's eyes flew open and she cried out, startled to find herself at the center of so many people.

With many platitudes, clichés and calming sigils, Renzo shepherded David and Rachel through the club and out to David's car.

Rachel, still dazed and confused by learning she had been unconscious on the bathroom floor, was all the way back to the silver Honda Accord before she realized someone was missing. "Gwen? Where's Gwen?"

"Get in the car," Renzo said urgently. "I'll explain everything later. Right now we need to get to a safe place."

CHAPTER 5

*R*enzo stormed around the living room of Gwen's apartment. David and Rachel sat huddled on the couch, watching his progress with wary eyes. The fiasco that had ended their evening was still a complete mystery to them, but a strong sense of self-preservation kept them silent as Renzo raged back and forth. At last he flopped into Gwen's favorite chintz chair and stared morosely at them.

"For the first time in my life, I don't know what to do." He glared at the two young mortals as if they were responsible for his dilemma. "I can't think straight until I know she's healed."

As he studied David and Rachel, emotions chased themselves through his mind. "Every instinct I have tells me to just wipe your memories and be done with it."

Their faces paled and their eyes widened with a mixture of fear and disbelief.

He sighed, closing his eyes. "But you're her friends, and you're going to need to understand what happened tonight to help her heal. Especially you, Rachel. She's going to need another woman she can talk to, someone she trusts, someone close at hand. Mei won't be around, and Gwen's more comfortable with you anyway."

He stopped as he realized he was thinking out loud, that his ramblings were only confusing the young mortals more than they already were.

Sighing again, Renzo scrubbed his face with his hands. "Look," he tried again, "I know this makes absolutely no sense to you, but will you trust me, and Gwen, just a little further? Will you promise to wait here in this apartment while I go and see how she's doing? I'll be back soon, and hopefully, I'll bring Gwen with me."

The pleading expression in his eyes erased Rachel's fears and she gave him a small smile and a nod of agreement.

David recognized Renzo's anguished concern for Gwen. How would he feel if he'd seen Rachel taken away battered and bruised and been unable to follow? He decided he could wait for answers — a least for a short while longer.

"We'll be here," David said quietly. "Bring her back safely... and then be prepared to give me some answers."

Renzo nodded gratefully, made an intricate motion with his right hand, and disappeared.

Rachel, who had not witnessed any of the events in the alley, gasped and clutched David's arm. Sensing his calm acceptance of the impossible, she stared into his eyes. "David, what's going on?"

Taking her in his arms and settling more comfortably into the sofa, he told her what little he knew.

CHAPTER 6

*R*enzo emerged in the overworld glade and ran to the shelter that had been erected under the spreading branches of the towering oak. Dylan met him at the entrance, holding out his hands.

"She's fine, Renzo," he said soothingly, "Merlin and Minerva have healed her physical hurts." He sighed and lowered his eyes. "Her psyche will take a little longer."

Renzo clenched his hands, then forced himself to relax them again. "Was there any physical damage to her mind? Or are we talking about shock, betrayal, and loss of trust?"

Dylan smiled grimly. "I hate to say it's *only* shock— that will certainly be hard enough to overcome— but no, no one actually invaded her mind with the intent of harming her. Her protective sigil wouldn't have allowed that."

"May I see her?"

"Of course, Renzo." Mei had quietly approached while the men stood talking. "Come with me."

She led him into the shelter, holding back a curtain to allow him access. Inside the quiet enclosure, Gwen lay curled in a fetal position on a mattress-sized pillow of down that floated a few feet off the ground. All signs of distress were gone, except for the tousled condition of her hair, and that could have been a normal consequence of restless sleep.

He brushed a strand of hair from her face and allowed a gentle tendril of thought to whisper across the edge of her consciousness. She was in a healing sleep. Nothing would disturb her until Minerva called her to wakefulness.

"Thank you, Mei." Renzo hugged her gently. He smiled ruefully at the unspoken question in her eyes. "I can't explain it, but I'm tied to her. I have to thank you for saving my life— for when you saved her, you saved me." He glance at Gwen again and rested his fingers on her wrist, needing to feel her steady pulse.

Mei took his other arm and gently pulled him from the healing area. "She will rest until she's awakened. Come, Renzo. You need to talk to Dylan about his findings."

Reassured by Gwen's peaceful slumber, Renzo allowed himself to be guided back to Dylan. As the two men sat down, they were joined by Merlin and Mei.

"Tell me everything you know," commanded Merlin. "Lady Guinevere obviously requires our protection."

Renzo and Dylan took it in turns to bring Merlin up to date on all the encounters between Gwen and Lilith and her minions. Renzo ended with a vivid description of Gwen's anguished scream and his unceremonious response. "I almost blasted her mortal friend, David Milligan, when he came running into the alley to rescue her. It's a good thing she was still conscious at that point. Speaking of which, I need to get back to David and Rachel — and I need guidance in knowing what to do about them."

Merlin nodded, his expression unreadable. "We'll leave that decision for a few moments. Dylan, have you interrogated the perpetrators?"

"Yes, Lord, I did."

"Was this a random crime, or were *Dark Old Ones* involved?"

"They were definitely guided by Lilith, Lord." Dylan closed his eyes and ordered his thoughts. "She hired them, gave them specific instructions about disabling Gwen, and told them how to lure her into the alley. She was actually present, waiting until she felt Gwen's presence in that hallway so that they would know the precise moment to spring their trap."

He glanced sympathetically at Renzo. "They were torturing a dog. Lilith knew that Gwen's sense of decency wouldn't allow her to ignore the animal's pain. As soon as they had her hands incapacitated, Lilith left. She evidently didn't feel the need to actually witness the rest of what was done to her."

He shuddered before continuing softly, "If they had rendered her unconscious before shattering her hands, we might have lost her."

There was a momentary silence while everyone contemplated the gruesome elegance of Lilith's plot.

Merlin broke the uneasy silence. "Fortunately for us, Lilith chooses to employ foul characters. They undoubtedly wanted her conscious in order to enjoy her terror. That's a vile thought, but in the end it's what saved her."

He was quiet again for a moment. "Any ideas why Lilith is so determined to kill Lady Guinevere?"

His question elicited only blank stares and puzzled contemplation.

Finally, Dylan spoke. "Gwen mentioned that at one of their early meetings Lilith mentioned a prophecy. Something she believes Gwen will fulfill."

Merlin looked up with interest. "Well, at least that gives us a direction. I'll have Sibyl look into it." He paused, looking closely at each of his companions. "It seems plain to me that Lilith has been testing the degree of High Magic's protection of Lady Guinevere. She has found the chink in the Light's armor. Gwen is susceptible to attack from a mortal if her magic can be disabled. We must decide how to repair this flaw. Suggestions?"

Renzo took a deep breath, held it for a few seconds and then spoke in a rush as he exhaled. "Lord Merlin, I'm not comfortable admitting this, but I think I'm... uhm... emotionally involved with the Lady Guinevere. I would like to ask your permission to leave my current assignment and move in with Gwen to protect her." He gazed defiantly at his colleagues, waiting for the expected outburst.

The other three merely smiled. Mei, at least, had the courtesy to attempt to hide her smile behind her hand.

Renzo's defiance turned to bewilderment. "What?" He eyed his friends warily.

Dylan made a vain attempt to project a serious facade, gave up and spoke as gently as possible. "Renzo, that's hardly news to us. Mei and I have had a bet going about how long it would take you to recognize your own symptoms. Of course, we would choose stronger terms than *emotionally involved*."

Merlin took charge of the conversation before Renzo could formulate a scathing reply. "You have my permission, Lord Lorenzo, though I believe you will need Lady Guinevere's as well... at least when it comes to your actual place of residence." His eyes twinkled with good-natured mischief.

"However, given what I overheard as she was being healed, I think she will have no serious objections." He smiled as he watched comprehension grow in Renzo's eyes. "Just be careful how you phrase your request, my lord. Women can be very touchy about such things."

Renzo blushed scarlet, and mumbled that he would be very careful indeed.

Merlin sobered quickly and wrapped up their impromptu council. "To summarize then, I will consult with Sibyl and ask her to join Mei, Dylan and myself in an exhaustive study of prophecy. We will try to determine which one Lady Guinevere is most likely to fulfill. We need to know what Lilith suspects."

The others nodded their agreement.

"Renzo will take on the responsibility of Guinevere's safety. I can't imagine a better a guardian for her. Now, to our last topic for consideration: what shall we do about her mortal friends?"

CHAPTER 7

*R*achel was amazed by the difference in Renzo's demeanor as he eased into Gwen's squashy chintz armchair. When he had left them a few minutes ago, he had been harassed and anxious, on the edge of a dangerous rage. Now he appeared relaxed and at peace, a gentle smile pulling at the corners of his mouth. She didn't know exactly what the change meant, but was certain it indicated Gwen was going to be fine.

When he'd returned, Renzo had brought a sleeping Gwen with him. The young woman now slumbered safely in her own bed. David and Rachel had been allowed to see her, to relieve their own worries, before being shepherded to the living area to talk to Renzo.

"Okay, here's the deal," Renzo said, "I'm going to tell you some unbelievable stuff, but then you've seen enough in the last few hours that it might not come as a shock." He paused to study their intent faces, and nodded as he seemed to find what he was looking for. "When I'm through, I'll give you some time to mull things over, but I won't allow you to leave this apartment until we've come to an understanding and you've made your choice."

"That sounds ominous," David said. "I'll tell you right now, I won't let you hurt Rachel. I don't care who or what you are."

Renzo smiled. "Relax, David. Neither of you is in any physical danger, it's just a matter of whether or not you choose to remember what I'm about to tell you after it's all said and done."

With that, he launched into a brief history of the race of *Old Ones* in general and Gwen in particular.

"So, let me see if I've got this straight." David sat forward, breaking the room's unnatural silence when Renzo finished. "You're an *Old One* and you can do magic. If Gwen's one too, why didn't she just blast those guys?"

"They knew who and what she was, and laid an intricate trap for her. They intended to kill her. Fortunately they missed a crucial step and I was able to intercede. I'll be on guard from now on."

The grim intent on his face was unmistakable.

"Renzo?" Rachel asked, her voice breathless, her pulse thundering in her ears. "She's still my friend, right? I mean, being an *Old One* hasn't changed her?"

Tears pricked her eyes and the edges of her vision darkened. She fought for control. She was strong enough to hear his answer.

"Rachel," he said gently, "Gwen was born an *Old One*. She is what she has always been. Nothing has changed between you."

Rachel stood, walked to the window, and stared at the park as early morning light stole across dew-sparkled grass.

"What were you saying about us making a choice?" David asked.

"While Gwen was being healed, several of us held a council. We decided that you should be told the truth about what happened.

She'd lost Gwen when they were children, and it had been a crushing blow.

But, according to Renzo, that had been this Lilith person's fault. Lilith had tried to kill Gwen when they were twelve... had succeeded in killing Gwen's parents.

All those years, Rachel had thought Gwen had died too. All because the other *Old Ones* had needed to hide Gwen in order to keep her safe.

Rachel jumped to her feet and paced the plush carpet. She could forget about this, go back to the easy ignorance she'd enjoyed the night before.

Yes. That was the answer.

Ignorance was bliss.

She stopped and hugged herself tightly, willing herself to think rationally, to not let fear make her choice.

No, ignorance wasn't bliss.

In this case it was cowardice.

Straightening her shoulders, Rachel strode to Gwen's dressing table and stared at her reflection.

Gwen would never willingly desert you," Rachel stated flatly, aring the woman in the mirror to disagree. The fire in her eyes ed as a thought flitted across her mind. *No, but she didn't tell you her. She didn't ask for your help.*

hing, Rachel returned to the bed and stroked Gwen's arm.

ourse she didn't tell me. She'd never put me in danger.

Renzo told me. Renzo asked for my help... and it was hard for him so. I don't think he's ever asked a mortal for help before.

You are to be allowed to decide whether or not you wish to be involved."

"Excuse me?"

Renzo scrubbed his face with his hands. "My initial reaction was to simply wipe your memory and send you home to your beds. I can still do that. You won't remember anything I've told you, or anything that happened last night other than that Gwen had an unfortunate accident in the alley. You'll know that she's physically fine, but a little traumatized."

Rachel walked back over to where they sat. "How does that help Gwen?"

Renzo studied her before answering. "It doesn't. She will continue to guard her secret life from you and will be forced to deal with her trauma without your support."

Rachel opened her mouth to protest, but Renzo spoke over her objections.

"Yes, I know, you'd still support her, knowing that she'd been a mugging victim— but she'd be unable to tell you her real fears, the true cause of her trauma."

Renzo turned to David, meeting his gaze squarely. "And you... you'd be unable to help protect her from future attacks. You'd believe it was a random mugging, and what are the odds of that happening again?"

David and Rachel stared at each other, then David looked at Renzo. "You want us to choose to remember, don't you?"

Renzo leapt from the chair and paced around the room. He stopped at the window near the spot Rachel had stood a few moments before.

"To be honest, I don't know what I want," he answered, staring through the glass with glazed eyes. "I want Gwen to be safe and whole. I know she has a better chance at that with both of us guarding her and Rachel fully aware of her situation."

He turned to face them and Rachel was surprised by the haggard look on his face.

"But I don't want to place you in danger, and I can't guarantee that you'll be safe." He stared at them, his expression anguished.

"The whole reason for our existence, the *Old Ones*, is to maintain the balance between good and evil, darkness and light. The reason we maintain that balance is to allow the human race to flourish and fulfill its destiny.

"Allowing you to place yourselves in the line of fire goes against everything I know, everything I am." His voice trailed off and he turned again to stare out the window.

David stood up and crossed the room to Renzo's side. Placing a hand on his shoulder, he said, "Count me in. Perhaps it's time a few of us humans lent a hand in the fight. I haven't known Gwen very long, but she's a friend and I know she's worthy of my protection. I can't say I understand the larger issues at stake, but I'm willing to do my part to protect her… and everyone else."

He smiled grimly. "I only wish I were trained in hand-to-hand combat. Fighting's not usually a necessity in an academic setting."

Renzo covered David's hand with his own. "You have a warrior's heart. Thank you."

"May I go sit with Gwen for a few minutes?" Rachel needed to escape from the testosterone permeating this room, to sit quietly by her friend's side and think.

David and Renzo turned to face her, and she was struck by the strong similarity in the set of their faces. His decision made, David was ready to do battle. She'd never seen this side of his personality before.

"Of course," Renzo said gently, "and Rachel," he continued when she paused on her way down the hall, "David's choice doesn't need to be yours."

Rachel nodded and practically ran down the hall. When she reached the sanctuary of Gwen's room, she clamped her mind against the impulse to bar the door and barricade herself inside with her sleeping friend. She sat despondently on the edge of the bed, taking Gwen's slack hand in her own. She wanted to cry, but knew that if she let down her emotional wall the result wouldn't be a civilized thing.

She could feel the howling, screeching lunatic that was her fe demanding release. The emotional demon inside her was gain strength; she fought against its seething mass of confus recognizing a few elements in the maelstrom: terror, a disappointment, and a liberal dose of resentment.

The resentment startled her, so she examined it more close

Ahh, there is was.

If she were honest she felt hurt and betrayed.

She'd thought Gwen was her friend, but the whole ti had been keeping this secret. She hadn't trusted Rachel tell her the truth.

Rachel shook her head and studied Gwen's sleeping fied her, how close she'd come to losing her friend l closed her eyes and tried to put her thoughts in ord

Smiling ruefully, Rachel patted Gwen's hand and, closing the bedroom door quietly behind herself, returned to the living room.

Renzo and David were deep in discussion of defensive tactics when Rachel reentered the room. She stood quietly for a moment watching them, their dark heads bent close together over a diagram of the museum David had drawn.

Her heart swelled with pride.

David was a good man, a dependable man... and just at that moment he was exhibiting a courage which she recognized as both rare and precious. He was fully aware that he was out of his depth, but he had chosen to stay and fight. She was proud of him, and of herself...

...because she knew she couldn't take the easy way out either.

CHAPTER 8

enzo spent the day getting to know all the nooks and crannies in Gwen's apartment, as well as the public areas of the building which housed it. He'd sent David and Rachel off early that morning with instructions to sleep and recuperate until the evening. He had no intention of waking Gwen from her healer-induced sleep until dinner time, and he wanted Rachel and David to be there when she awoke to support her with their love and concern.

He also coveted their aid in getting himself established in her life. He figured three against one— and that one dazed and defenseless— were good odds.

Promptly at 7:00 p.m. the doorbell rang and Renzo rushed to answer its summons. Rachel and David stepped into the apartment looking refreshed, though a little apprehensive. Renzo greeted them warmly and led them to Gwen's bedroom.

"Right," he said, "let's get on with it. Rachel, why don't you sit on the bed beside her? David, you stand over here by the door, and

I'll..." his voice trailed off as he tried to decide where he should be.

Rachel cocked her head and said, "Renzo, you need to be right here beside her." She moved to the other side of her sleeping friend and sat tailor fashion on the blue and white coverlet. "She'll need to see you as soon as she wakes up. Go ahead," she urged, "sit on the edge of the bed. That's right."

Renzo sat a little gingerly, all too aware of the two mortals in the room. He picked up Gwen's hand and held it tightly in his left hand while he traced the sigil Minerva had taught him with his right.

Instantly Gwen's eyes popped open... and she screamed, drawing her body into a tight ball. Pulling her hand away from Renzo with a violence that startled her friends, she threw an energy shield around herself.

Rachel scrambled toward the far edge of the bed, anxiously putting some distance between herself and the crackling blue field that swirled around her friend.

David leapt from the door and supported Rachel as she clung precariously to the side of the bed.

Renzo sat perfectly still, his face deceptively calm, his eyes closed.

Gwen, Renzo called, tentatively reaching out to her mind with a tendril of thought. *You're safe, Gwen. Open your mind to me. It's Renzo. No one here will harm you.*

He bathed her consciousness with the warmth of his love. A love he was only now beginning to recognize for what it was. He sent a calming thought to Rachel and wove her love and concern into his own, creating a blanket of warmth and comfort. Finally, he added David's strength and support, and the emotional fabric solidified.

Come back to us, Gwen, he whispered at the edge of her soul. *We're here for you.*

Open your eyes, my love. His thought became more urgent as he sensed her slight movement.

That's right, sweetheart. Look at me... it's Renzo and Rachel and David. You can lower your shield. You're safe here.

At last Gwen peered through the blue haze of her defensive spell and recognized her friends, saw that she was in her own bedroom. She raised her head, looked at Renzo, touched his mind to be sure he was real, and dropped her shield.

Renzo quickly gathered her in his arms as a deep sob wracked her body.

"Are you really here?" she cried. "Is it truly over? My hands!"

She ripped herself from his embrace and stared at her hands. After examining them carefully, she gazed at Renzo in confusion.

"Surely I didn't dream what happened," she said, near hysteria, "I couldn't have dreamed something that horrible."

"It was no dream, Gwen," Renzo told her calmly. "It happened, and I'm so sorry I wasn't there to protect you."

His face paled. His guard was down; her terror and confusion battered his mind, but he refused to close their link, continuing to wrap her in the warmth of their love and support.

"But you came... you were there." Her eyes filled with tears . "You saved me. I don't remember much, but I know my hands were..." She gave a violent shudder at the remembered pain. "...and then you were there, and I was safe."

"Your hands are fine, Gwen." Rachel's calm voice floated into her consciousness as if from another world. "The *Old Ones* healed you. You've been asleep all day. Renzo brought you home to us this morning."

"You're strong, Gwen," David said, "you can handle this. We'll help you. Rachel and me. You're not alone anymore."

Gwen froze in Renzo's arms. Slowly, she lifted her eyes and looked at Rachel and David. Rachel moved closer. David smiled reassuringly.

"*Old Ones?*" Gwen repeated in alarm. "You know about *Old Ones?*"

Rachel smiled and took one of Gwen's hands in her own. "Renzo told us all about them— and you."

Before Gwen could respond, Renzo spoke up, "It's okay, Gwen. Merlin has agreed that Rachel and David need to know what's going on. I told them everything and gave them the option to forget." He paused to brush a strand of hair from her eyes. "They chose to remember."

Tears gathered in Gwen's eyes, and Renzo reluctantly released her to Rachel's embrace. He stood, met David's gaze over the women's heads, and the two men tactfully withdrew.

CHAPTER 9

*G*wen rested comfortably in the circle of Renzo's arms. David had taken Rachel home an hour ago over her protests that she couldn't possibly leave Gwen with the kitchen in such a mess. Renzo had quietly produced a cleaning sigil, and Rachel's protests had died with a small "Oh!" of astonishment.

The television droned in the background as the weatherman attempted to forecast the next week's weather. Renzo slept lightly, his head thrown back on the couch in relaxed abandon.

Gwen sighed. It was true. Everything was all right. The horrors of the alley were in the past, her hands were whole, and life was as it should be. She snuggled closer to Renzo, enjoying his physical proximity. She didn't know how long he would stay; they hadn't discussed the issue. It was enough that he was here now.

Her thoughts skirted carefully around the edges of her recent trauma. She knew she would have to examine those memories soon. It wasn't safe to allow them to fester. They would hold too much power over her future actions if she ignored them... but for right now, for this precious space of time she could simply bask in the knowledge that Renzo had come for her.

She had cried out mindlessly, and he had responded with an answering recklessness. He had not stopped to count the cost; had not stayed to study the situation. He had simply known she needed him and thrown himself into unknown peril for her sake. She hugged that knowledge tightly to her heart as her eyes drowsed closed.

RENZO WOKE to find Gwen sleeping snugly in the crook of his arm. He gently stroked the silk-soft mass of her hair and then picked up the hand that lay quietly curled on his chest. A vivid image of that same hand, shattered and swollen, flashed before his mind's eye.

He shied from the memory and forced himself to concentrate on the hand he held— whole and firm, with no trace of recent injury. He tightened his grip on her lithe young body and thanked the Creator and High Magic that he had been in time, that she had sustained no lasting harm.

Gwen stirred at the intensity of his hug, and he forced himself to relax.

This was all he wanted… to sit in front of the TV with the woman he loved asleep in his arms.

His breath caught. He hadn't admitted that before, not even to himself. Well, he'd just have to get used to the thought.

He loved Gwen.

He. Loved. Gwen.

And since everyone else seemed to know it already, he might as well say the words aloud to her as well.

But the older, more cynical side of his mind disagreed. He was ancient. She was a baby. It didn't matter if he loved her, she was too young to be anything other than infatuated. And infatuation never lasted.

And even if she did harbor some infantile idea of love being a forever thing, she had no idea just how long forever could be. He did. And he didn't relish nursing a broken heart for eternity.

Better never to admit to his feelings than to allow their love to grow... only to be devastated when it didn't last.

He needed to leave things alone. He could protect her without asking for her love.

He squirmed on the sofa, suddenly uncomfortable with the whole situation. Okay, so he wasn't Prince Charming, and he wasn't going to get the girl. That wasn't exactly a news flash. He'd been around a long time, and except for his first love— back before he'd known he was immortal— he'd managed to stay sane and keep his heart safe.

This was just a little more complicated. Gwen was an immortal too. Her life span would match his— assuming he could deal with Lilith's malice. Any other women he'd been interested in during his long existence had been mortal, and he'd been all too clear on exactly *why* there'd been no future in such a liaison.

So what if this relationship had potential where others had not? That still didn't mean it was going anywhere. It simply meant it was more dangerous than any other attraction he'd ever felt.

He'd really have to watch himself with Gwen. This attraction was emotional quicksand.

Gwen interrupted his thought process by stretching and sitting up.

"I fell asleep again," she said, stating the obvious.

Renzo didn't reply; silence stretched between them.

Gwen waited a few moments before asking, "So, what do we do now? Will you stay with me until I find the next sign? I mean, Lughnasadh is only three days from now."

Renzo roused himself from the cynical cycle his thoughts were caught in and glanced at her in surprise. "What? Of course, I'll stay."

Then he remembered that he still hadn't talked to her about his reassignment as her bodyguard.

Right. He needed to approach this carefully. Remembering Merlin's warning, he considered his words. The last thing he wanted was to upset her.

"Gwen," he began, "please don't take this the wrong way." He hesitated, thinking he'd already blown his presentation.

"What I mean is... well, I'm going to be here full time. I've been reassigned. I'm your official bodyguard now."

Her expression flitted from joy to wounded to a carefully neutral mask in a matter of seconds.

"Oh," she said quietly, lowering her gaze to study her hands, "what does that mean? You've been reassigned?"

Quicksand, be damned, he thought savagely. He couldn't bear to see that guarded expression on her face. Not when she was talking to him!

He had no choice. He had to tell her the truth. If he got hurt, he'd deal.

"I phrased that badly."

Placing a finger under her chin, raised her face to his. "I pretty much demanded that Merlin allow me to abandon my current project so I could be with you full time— to protect you."

A radiant smile spread across her face; he couldn't have misinterpreted the look in her eyes if he'd tried.

She loved him, too.

Neither of them had said the words, but a warm glow melted the ice of his earlier cynicism.

He'd found his soul-mate, and he sure as hell wasn't going to let Lilith take her away from him.

"If it's all right with you, I'd like to stay here. Of course, if you're not comfortable with that, I can arrange to make the apartment next door available."

She giggled, her face glowing. "I don't think we need to disrupt Mr. Allenby's life." She sat still for another moment and then launched herself into his arms. "Oh, Renzo. I'm so happy. This is wonderful... and Merlin has agreed to let you come here?"

He hugged her tightly, enjoying the sensations produced by having her healthy young body pressed firmly against his own. Forcing himself to think, he pushed her away gently and told her everything the impromptu counsel of *Old Ones* had discussed.

"So," he concluded, "you can tell Rachel anything you want. She and David have freely chosen to ally themselves with the Light. David will help me protect you by keeping an eye on you at the museum, and by alerting us to any suspicious sorts who might take undue interest in you at work. Merlin, Dylan and Mei are studying the prophecy connection, and I'm in charge of watching your back at all other times."

He smiled and gave her a sly wink. "Not what I'd call an unpleasant task."

She blushed, and he laughed outright.

"Everything is in place now. Tomorrow I'm going to check out this professor who's been giving you a hard time." He glared at her as she started to protest. "Your only jobs are to find the next clue, find the Lughnasadh sign, and do your homework... in that order."

Gwen saluted briskly, her dark eyes sparkling. "Yes, sir."

Her expression sobered as she took his hand. When she spoke, her voice was husky with emotion. "I haven't really thanked you." She placed a finger on his lips to still his reply .

"Thank you for my life, Lorenzo. Thank you for your willingness to stay and guard me." She leaned forward and kissed him. Not a passionate kiss, but a tender one, sealing a bargain and promising a rich harvest in due season.

"You're very welcome." Renzo savored the sensations her kiss produced, reveling in the knowledge that they were only an appetizer. The feast would come in due time.

He was a patient man.

He could wait while she healed.

CHAPTER 10

Gwen woke to a surge of adrenaline. Air rushed into her lungs in a wheezing gasp, and she had to press both hands over her mouth to stifle the resultant ear-piercing shriek.

Her hands!

She yanked them from her face and tried to examine them in the dark room. They worked fine. They didn't hurt.

That wasn't enough information; she needed to see that they weren't the swollen masses of shattered bone and cartilage she'd been dreaming about.

Fumbling awkwardly in the blackness, Gwen finally managed to connect with the bedside lamp and bathe the room in blessed light.

Surveying her room, she saw that while her hands were whole and strong, her bed was not. The sheets and light summer blanket were wrapped around her legs in an intricate knot. It was no wonder she had been dreaming of captivity. Even the fitted bottom sheet had been worried loose at one corner. It was a good thing she'd had all that ensorcelled sleep the day before, she certainly hadn't been resting so far tonight.

Slowly, Gwen's heart rate regulated and her breathing quieted. She was safe in her own room. Her hands were healed. There weren't even any scars to bear witness to the brutality she had endured. At least, there weren't any scars on her hands. The bed's disarray testified to the emotional scars she was still dealing with, would be dealing with for some time yet.

Gwen shivered, not from chill, but from nerves, and forced herself to her feet. If only she could straighten her emotions as easily as she straightened the tangled bedding. As she worked at remaking the bed, she tried to distract herself from her psychic wounds by thinking about Renzo.

Renzo.

Her knight in shining armor.

He'd rescued her. He'd thrown himself into unknown danger to save her. Her heart swelled with gratitude. Her hands stopped their mechanical smoothing of sheets and she stood still.

No, it was much more than gratitude. It was definitely love.

Guinevere Enid Vaughan loved Lorenzo Alan Santini.

It was as simple as that ... at least in her own heart. It undoubt- edly wouldn't be simple in the real world, but at this moment, the real world didn't count. What mattered was the truth inside herself.

She loved him, and though the words hadn't been spoken, she knew Renzo loved her as well. His actions spoke much louder than any words could. Not only had he saved her from— her thoughts shied away from exactly what he had saved her from—

but he had woven and held the love and support that had allowed her to awaken to sanity.

Gwen glanced at the clock.

3:00 a.m.

Much too early to be up. Dutifully she crawled back between the newly tucked sheets. Closing her eyes, she willed herself to relax and rest. As soon as she released control of her conscious mind, her subconscious filled the gap with the voices of the men who had hurt her. She heard again in graphic detail all the horrifying, sexually perverted acts they had planned to execute on her body. She felt again the acute terror of knowing that she was absolutely powerless to prevent her own torture, incapable of expediting her inevitable death. A quick clean death was far superior to the painful rending and tearing of body and soul they had in mind for her.

Her eyes flew open, and turning on the lights, Gwen jumped from the bed. She paced the perimeter of the room, arms wrapped tightly around her body to control its tremors. At last she stopped in front of her dressing table and stared at her reflection in the mirror.

I am safe. They didn't do any of those things to me. I will not let them control my thoughts. She glared at herself, silently acknowledging the rage that was building in her soul. *I will not let them defile my love for Renzo. When the time comes, I will have sex and I will NOT be afraid. Lilith will NOT win.*

As quickly as it flared, the defiance left her. Gwen looked at the bed out of the corner of her eye. She wouldn't let them win, but she didn't have to claim a complete victory right this minute.

For now, there was no way she was getting back into that bed.

Decision made, she put on her robe and slippers and headed to the kitchen. If she couldn't sleep, then she would cook. She'd banish the ghosts with the wholesome smells of banana nut bread and maple walnut French toast.

CHAPTER 11

*T*ousle-headed and groggy, Renzo wandered into the kitchen following his nose in search of the coffee whose aroma had penetrated his slumber. He found Gwen transferring a stack of pancakes from the stove to a table laden with enough food to feed them for a week.

"Wow," he said peering bleary-eyed at the heavily laden table, "do you eat like this every morning?"

Her cheeks blossomed in a very becoming shade of pink and she bit her lower lip.

His grogginess disappeared in a heart-beat as he fought down a primitive urge to take over that task. Biting that succulent lower lip of hers was a much more inviting prospect than sampling the breakfast treats arrayed before him.

Oh yeah, he'd be happy to sample anything she offered.

Grimacing, he forced himself to examine the food on the table.

Down boy. Remember the terror in her eyes last night? It's going to take some time before she's ready to offer you anything other than food. That was a nasty experience. Chancing a glance at her face, he saw her gold-rimmed brown eyes lower demurely. *Yeah, but that doesn't mean I can't dream.*

"I didn't know what you like for breakfast," she said, as he forced his attention back to the current conversation, "so I just fixed everything I could think of. I sure hope you're not a 'coffee only' kind of guy."

"I'm certainly not when a feast like this is available. Let's eat."

She laughed delightedly as he attacked a plate of French toast then reached for the platter of bacon and scrambled eggs.

GWEN NIBBLED an oat scone while she watched Renzo eat.

He was here.

In her kitchen, eating food she had prepared with her own hands. He'd slept in her guest bedroom, under a quilt her mother had made.

He'd've slept in her bed if she'd given him any encouragement. But her heart had nearly stopped at the thought of allowing any man, even her beloved Renzo, into her bed.

Renzo had immediately dropped his playful banter, hugged her tenderly— and gracefully accepted the room next to hers.

He was here.

He cared for her... and he wasn't going away anytime soon.

Gwen sighed, her heart content...

...but by the middle of the morning, her contentment had stretched dangerously thin

The man insisted on accompanying her everywhere.

At first it was sweet. He strolled along beside her on the way to class, carrying her books like an adolescent with his first crush. The irritation began when he insisted on coming into her first lecture.

"This is ridiculous, no one is going to bother me in class. Lilith doesn't like witnesses." She stood rooted to the sidewalk in front of the Linguistics building, her eyes darting from Renzo to the heavy glass doors. Other students were hurrying through those doors on their way to classrooms. She glanced at her watch, then at his face. She needed to get through that door, but was determined not to move until he backed off.

His level gaze held no trace of his usual mischievous twinkle. "Save your breath. I'm coming in." The twinkle returned as he allowed a small smile to play around the corners of his mouth. "No one will see me, I'll use the *I'm not here, don't pay attention to me* sigil. You know how well that one works.

"As for Lilith not wanting witnesses, you know perfectly well she wouldn't bat an eyelash at killing everyone on campus if she thought it would serve her main purpose... eliminating you."

Her resistance deflated and she heaved a weary sigh. With a quick nod of agreement she strode toward the double glass doors. "Come on, then. You're right, of course. I'm not the only one in danger. I need to take the lives of all these innocents into consideration."

She threw him a pleading look as he dragged the heavy door open. "But... please stay at the back of the room. I really need to concentrate in this class."

He nodded, trying— and failing— to suppress a grin, stepped into an alcove, and produced the sigil.

Gwen could still see him, but knew from her experience with Aunt Katie that no one else would notice him. In fact, as the professor droned on, she discovered that Renzo began to fade from her own awareness... at least when her attention wasn't focused on him. That was a definite plus, because his presence in the room was a huge distraction. Her face lit briefly in a secret smile.

He was here.

He cared for her.

The rest of the day rattled along in a similar fashion. Gwen's surface irritation at being treated like a preschooler was real, but deep inside she was profoundly grateful for his reassuring presence. Nothing would harm her while Renzo was on guard.

He was more than a bodyguard, he was her talisman of safety against mortal danger. High Magic had provided a sigil to protect her against dark magic, now Renzo's love completed her circle of security, protecting her from mortal interference.

Renzo released his *I'm not here* sigil after her last class and walked beside her openly as they meandered through the park to her part-time job. Totally absorbed in their conversation, she was relaxed and at ease when they arrived at the museum.

As they stepped through the outer doors, David burst from the entrance hall into the relative privacy of the airlock entrance.

"Where have you been?"

He towered over her, glaring, fists jammed against hips; his agitation so fierce, it bordered on rage.

Gwen reacted to his emotional barrage on instinct alone.

CHAPTER 12

*T*he blood drained from her face as Gwen took an involuntary step back. She raised her hands in a reflexive action, preparing an offensive sigil.

"Stop." Renzo pulled her into his arms and forced her hands still by the simple expedient of crushing them between their bodies.

Gwen fought his controlling arms with a strength she didn't know she possessed. She would have won her freedom if the soothing tendrils of his mind-voice hadn't finally found their way into her conscious mind. She felt the warmth of his love in those quiet thoughts, and allowed herself to relax in his arms.

David paled, stunned at the reaction he'd caused.

"God! Gwen, I'm so sorry. I didn't think. I've been on edge all day." Rocking back on his heels and unclenching his fists, he fixed Renzo with a chagrined look. "Is she all right? I'm so sorry."

Before Renzo could answer, Gwen surprised them all by giggling. Renzo looked down at her and cautiously relaxed his grip. She lifted her head to smile reassuringly at him and stepped free of his arms.

Turning to face David she gave another little chortle. "We're quite a pair. You need to chill out, and I need…" she took a deep breath, gave a small shudder and continued, "I need to remember who my friends are."

The smile she gave him was a little shaky, but sincere. "You're sorry you scared me, and I'm sorry I nearly blasted you."

She took Renzo's hand and held it in both of hers. "Thank you. David has no idea how close he came to serious injury. Thanks for saving us both."

Renzo took her by the arms and drew her into a bear hug. "You're amazing. You're going to be just fine." He smiled at David over the top of her head. "Let this be a lesson to you: don't put her in a position where she feels threatened. At least, not for the next few weeks."

David took a deep breath, held it for an instant, then expelled it with a groaning sigh. "Right. I'll behave. I'll even try not to hover. Just… promise you'll yell if you need me."

Gwen relaxed as Renzo's arms released her. She grinned at David. "You bet, I will. I'm fine… now. I appreciate your help, and your concern." She turned to Renzo. "I guess I'll see you later, then?"

He smiled. "I'll be waiting right here when your shift is over." A thought whispered at the edge her consciousness. *I'm here. Call me if you need me.*

I will. Suddenly, she was at peace. The soft caress of his thoughts soothed her in ways she couldn't explain.

With a shiver of happiness, Gwen roused herself. Taking David by the arm, she headed through the door and toward her work station. "Come on. Let's get some work done."

Gwen hummed happily as she catalogued a collection of African artifacts, so engrossed in examining the Maasai shield and spear currently on her table that she didn't even notice David walk past for the fourth time in two hours.

She could almost smell the dust and see the heat shimmer of the African plains as she stroked the shaft of the spear. The wood was smooth and worn where the tribesman had gripped it in preparation for a killing strike. She wondered idly how many lions and hyenas had met their death at the point of this efficient weapon. The Maasai cattle herds would have been well protected by a warrior wielding this spear. She hoped the shield had been as effective at guarding him.

Running her fingers lightly over the surface of the shield, Gwen detected a small flaw in the stitching which held it together. Leaning closer, she saw a small sigil begin to glow around the rough spot on the leather. The melody she'd been humming died a quick death as her breath caught.

Glancing swiftly around, she saw David watching her from a work station three cubicles down. A discreet crook of her finger gave him the signal he'd clearly been hoping for. Before she could even organize her thoughts, he'd pulled up a chair and sat beside her.

"What's up?"

She glanced around the large open room again, noticing where the other occupants were working. To avoid drawing their attention, she pitched her voice to carry only a few feet. "I think I've just found the clue to the Lughnasadh sign."

David stared at her blankly. "The what sign?"

"Sorry, I thought Renzo told you about my quest. Lughnasadh is an *Old One* High Day."

His frown deepened.

"A day when magic power is greater. Anyway, Lughnasadh is August first— day after tomorrow— and I have to find a sign on that day. One of these." She held up her hand so that the signs on her charm bracelet tinkled softly against each other. "The signs are hidden all around the world, so I'm given a clue about where to look each time." She gestured to the shield. "I think I've just found my next clue."

"Cool. How do you find out for sure?" His liquid brown eyes sparkled with excitement.

"I'm going to activate the sigil." She sighed at the look of total perplexity on his face. "Just stand there and shield me from the rest of the room. Try to keep anyone from coming over for a couple of minutes."

While she spoke, she pulled out a sheet of clean paper and made sure her pen was functioning. Flashing him a smile, she said, "Don't worry. I'm not even sure you'll be able to see anything."

Then she closed her eyes, took a deep breath, and forgot that David, or any of their colleagues, existed.

When she was sufficiently calm and grounded, she opened her eyes and touched the glowing symbol with her index finger. As she had expected, words suddenly sang in her mind and she raced to write them down before the song ended. The words reverberated in her brain for a few moments, chasing each other across her neural pathways.

Finally, her pen stopped moving, the words stopped singing, and the light of the sigil extinguished itself.

With a sigh, Gwen ran her fingers over the leather where the sigil had been. The anomaly was gone. The sigil's magic had healed the flaw as it departed.

After folding the paper and stowing it in her backpack, Gwen looked up at David, who was still warily watching the other people milling about in the large workroom. "It's okay. I'm finished."

"Was it your clue?" He glanced down at her and then looked at the shield and spear laying on the table.

"Yep, it sure was. Why don't you and Rachel come over for dinner tonight? We can all work on figuring out what the clue means." Gwen smiled, relieved to know the poem was safely in her backpack.

She could hardly wait to tell Renzo.

CHAPTER 13

The four friends sat around Gwen's dining table, the air redolent with the comforting fragrance of garlic and tomato. The lasagna and salad had been devoured and the table was now littered with the congenial clutter of a well-enjoyed meal. Renzo tossed his red and white linen napkin on the table and groaned. "Now that was a meal."

Rachel smiled sweetly. "Glad you enjoyed it. Mama Rosa has never let me down yet."

"Take-out Italian is definitely a lifesaver on busy days," Gwen added, stretching blissfully.

David jumped to his feet, rubbed his hands together and fixed Gwen with a challenging stare. "Wonderful. We're full, we're relaxed... let's get to the clue. I've been patient long enough. Aren't you curious about what it says?"

Gwen laughed. "I know what it says; I wrote it down, remember? But, you're right; I don't know what it means. Time to get to work."

Rachel hopped up and started to stack the dirty dishes. "You three get started. I'll just clean up the kitchen."

Renzo laid a restraining hand on her arm and chuckled. "Allow me." He traced a sigil with a flourish and the dishes leapt from Rachel's hands.

She quickly resumed her seat, barely avoiding several pieces of flying cutlery, and narrowed her eyes at Renzo. "Show off. Just because you can use magic doesn't mean you need to do so for every little chore."

He stared at her, eyes wide with assumed innocence. "I'm just saving you from household drudgery." His face assumed a hurt puppy expression. "I thought you'd be pleased."

When her expression changed from wary to alarmed, he relented and gave her his most charming smile. "Okay, next time you can do the dishes, but right now, we need your input in deciphering this clue."

Rachel clenched her right fist, her face reddening. "If Gwen and David weren't waiting for us, I'd be tempted to punch you, but I'll resist the temptation for now." She pasted a simpering smile on her face. "After all, for some unknown reason, Gwen likes you."

Renzo choked on a laugh, and followed as Rachel strode from the kitchen.

David and Gwen had made good use of their time. Gwen had produced a whiteboard and easel and David had retrieved the folded paper from the outside pocket of her backpack. As Renzo and Rachel made themselves comfortable on the couch and love seat, respectively, David read the rhyme aloud so Gwen could copy it on the board.

When she finished writing, Gwen sat next to Renzo and they all surveyed the words.

Seven Signs make a Sigil.
Seven Continents make the World.
Each Continent harbors one Sign,
Bringing balance to the globe.

Lughnasadh holds power.
Seek the Sign of Earth then.
Come to the Roof of Africa
The rain forest protects the sign.

Renzo studied the words carefully. "Well, this is certainly different from the other three. It doesn't rhyme, and there's not much meter."

"True," said Gwen, "but we're not really interested in its poetic merits. Only its meaning."

"It has meaning?" Rachel gave Gwen a puzzled look. "What's that first word in the second stanza? I've never seen it before. Do you know how to pronounce it?"

Gwen smiled at her friend. "It's the name of a specific Arcane High Day."

Rachel's eyes took on a distinct deer-in-the-headlights expression.

"Think of it as an *Old One* holiday," Gwen explained. "There are eight. This one is pronounced Loo-nah-sah."

"Do you think it's related to lunacy?" David quipped.

"It certainly could be. Especially the way you mortals chose to celebrate it in ancient times." Renzo scowled as he remembered stories he'd read in the Gramarye library. "Would you believe the ancient Celts used to kill their king at Lughnasadh? Wonderful idea, that. Kill the strongest or smartest man in your tribe. Great way to insure your culture's survival. But, we're off the subject."

"Right. Gwen explained signs and sigils to me, so I get the first line." Rachel's face was intent as she studied the words on the whiteboard.

David settled onto the love seat close to Rachel and absentmind-edly draped his arm across her shoulders. "Well, the rest of that stanza seems pretty clear. You're supposed to find one sign on each continent. Has that been true so far?" He looked directly at Gwen as he waited for her answer.

"Let me think." She idly fingered the signs on her bracelet, staring unseeingly at the coffee table. "The first sign was in Idaho. That's North America."

"Duh," said David, "Do you think?"

Renzo sent him a scathing look. "Shut up and let her think. You're the one who asked the question."

Gwen ignored them both. She touched the sign of wind and continued. "The second was at the top of Mt. Everest. That's Asia, isn't it?"

She glanced at Rachel for confirmation; the petite blonde had always been a whiz at geography. Rachel nodded.

"The third came from the Rock of Gibraltar. That must be Europe, though it's really close to Africa... right across the Strait of Gibraltar."

"Yes, Gibraltar's part of Europe," Renzo confirmed. "So far, we're three continents for three signs."

"Wait a minute," David interrupted, "you already knew you were supposed to look for one of these things on Lughnasadh. You told me that before you even knew what the clue said. So why the reference to Lughnasadh?"

"It's just a confirmation that this is the right clue for this moment. The signs can only be found at their appointed time. It wouldn't do her any good to look for the Lughnasadh sign at Beltane." Renzo replied.

"So, the really important stuff is in the last two lines?" Rachel asked.

"Certainly looks that way." Renzo nodded his agreement. "We really don't care which element the sign represents, but we definitely need to know where to look."

Gwen let their conversation flow over her as she thought about the information contained in the lines before her. "This sign is in Africa," she said to no one in particular. "In the rain forest." Her eyes widened and she looked at her friends with excitement. "The second clue called Mt. Everest 'The Roof of the World'... do you suppose 'the Roof of Africa' is a mountain?"

"Good thought," said Renzo, "but it's not a name I'm familiar with. Either of you ever heard the phrase?"

David and Rachel shook their heads. Then David bounced up and strode to Gwen's desk. He sat in her secretarial chair and powered up her computer.

"Let's do an Internet search for the phrase." He turned to grin at them. "You can find anything on the Internet."

The others crowded around him as he quickly tapped out his request in the search engine. The machine whirred happily for an instant and returned a full page of web sites listing references to "roof of Africa."

Scanning down the list, they found that all the sites that referenced the whole phrase— as opposed to an individual word— mentioned Kilimanjaro. Africa's tallest mountain and one of the highest free-standing mountains in the world.

To Gwen's delight, they learned that Kilimanjaro's lower slopes were covered by rain forest.

"Well," she said with a satisfied smile, "that certainly narrows the field. I'll be searching the slopes of Kilimanjaro for this sign. Tanzania, here I come."

CHAPTER 14

*L*ughnasadh.

Gwen could almost feel the crackle of magic against her skin when she woke on the first of August. She rubbed her arms briskly, watching the lines of power dance in response to her action. Either she was more aware, or this was an unusually powerful day... even for an Arcane High Day. Gwen bounced out of bed and hurried through her morning routine, anxious to get her quest accomplished so she wouldn't be late to her first class.

It wasn't until she was in the shower that the realization hit her.

She felt rested.

She had slept peacefully through the night.

Gwen stood in the tub, hot water stinging her unprotected flesh with fiery needles, and gloried in her release from night terror. All her senses were fully awake— not like the last few mornings when she'd felt muddled; dazed by lack of sleep. Even the soap lathering her hands smelled crisper, more pungent.

She wondered briefly if the raw power of heightened magic was responsible for her release.

Whatever. She felt great and had no intention of worrying about why.

Stepping from the shower and wrapping herself in a soft, white towel, she inhaled the delicate fragrance of her favorite lavender-scented fabric softener. Breathing deeply, she savored the fragrance before exhaling with a satisfied sigh.

This was going to be a glorious day!

Renzo was already dressed and eating a bagel when Gwen entered the kitchen. The warm, golden glow of the early morning sun bathed him in a subtle luster. He might not be wearing armor, but seeing him framed in that light made Gwen realize yet again: he was her shining knight.

"I thought you'd be up early." He smiled and handed her a freshly toasted bagel dripping with butter and honey. "Do you want coffee or milk?"

"Milk, please." She took the bagel and gave him a quick kiss on the cheek. "Good morning." Her heart singing, she moved to the table and perched on a chair.

Renzo's eyes followed her closely as he retrieved the milk from the refrigerator and poured a glass. He moved quickly and efficiently around her kitchen, joining her at the table before she was well settled.

"You're very chipper this morning. Did you rest well?" Though they hadn't discussed it, Renzo was acutely aware that she hadn't been sleeping. He'd decided it was better to respect her privacy and wait for her to broach the subject.

Gwen surprised him with a dazzling smile, the kind he hadn't seen on her face since before the attack. Its return made his heart swell in his chest. She was healing, and faster than he would have guessed possible.

"I feel wonderful. I don't know if it's the extra magic in the air or what, but I slept soundly all night. Not a single bad dream."

"That's wonderful. Congratulations." He took another bite of his bagel.

They ate in comfortable silence, each enjoying the bright promise of this magical morning.

When Gwen had licked the last bit of honey from her fingers and swallowed the final gulp of her milk, Renzo broke the silence. "What's your plan? Do you want to wait for a threshold time? Or do you want to seek now?"

"My instinct is to go now. There's so much magic crackling in the air around us, I can't imagine it'll be necessary to wait for noon or twilight." She fixed him with a penetrating gaze. "Do you know of any reason to choose one time over another?"

He looked startled at the question. "None at all. This is your quest. Your instincts are the ones that count." He reached across the table to stroke her hand. "The only interference you'll get from me is over security concerns... and I don't think we're going to clash about that anymore."

She intertwined her fingers with his. "No, we're in complete agreement about the need for caution. In fact," she felt a shiver run down her spine as she met his gaze, "we've come into agreement on a lot of issues in the last few days."

"Harmony is a beautiful thing." Renzo licked his lips, his voice suddenly husky and dry. "When you're ready, I'd like to test that harmony in more physical terms."

Gwen lowered her gaze, her cheeks flaring deep rose. Her breath came fast and shallow, and she felt a little light-headed. She surprised herself by answering him quietly, "I'd like that too, but not quite yet."

"I can wait." He squeezed her hand, stroking it with his thumb. "I've waited centuries for you, a few more weeks, or even months, won't matter." They sat quietly for a few moments, their joined hands their only point of contact.

At last, Gwen gave a small shake and raised her eyes to meet his. "I like the direction this conversation has taken." She smiled at him, her eyes liquid and dreamy. "But right now, I have a job to do. Shall we get started?"

Reluctantly, he released her hand and gave her a small nod. "As you wish, milady."

Rising from the table, Gwen walked to the middle of her living room and looked speculatively at her surroundings. "The seeking usually doesn't take very long, so I don't think I need to bother getting comfortable."

She had trouble concentrating as she watched Renzo approach. He was just so... male. Her senses, unusually acute this morning, were filled by his presence. The scent of him... spicy with a sensual muskiness. His voice overwhelmed every other sound, echoing through her very soul. The imprint of his fingers lingered on her hand, her blood carrying his heat all the way to her heart.

What would he taste like? Morning coffee and bagel would linger on his lips. What an intoxicating combination: coffee, bagel and Renzo.

She turned away to face the window. The sight of the lines of power arcing across his body was overpowering. She'd need to maintain some distance from him until her physical receptors returned to their normal state.

"I'd like to do more than maintain a mind-touch this time."

Renzo stood right behind her. She felt his presence, though he hadn't touched her. Keeping her back to him, she stepped closer to the window, widening the gap between them. "What do you have in mind?"

He closed the distance, and wrapped her in his arms. "This."

Gwen's world exploded.

The intensity with which their fields of power melded simultaneously robbed her of breath and threw her violently into the gelatinous bubble.

She was aware of Renzo's electrified confusion, but had no time to think about it. She had to control the scintillating whirlwind of power before it ejected them into who-knew-what place or time.

Renzo tightened his grip around her waist as she fought to manipulate and regulate the power raging around her. Gradually, it came under her control and she was able to direct her search. She forced her will upon the swirling inferno, and turned her attention to the African continent. She sought through the brooding maelstrom for the golden glow which would guide her to the sign.

There.

With a profound sense of elation, she threw herself, and Renzo, out of the bucking, surging power and onto the slopes of Kilimanjaro.

The moment they materialized, Gwen turned in Renzo's arms and attacked him with a kiss so primal and passionate that his heart almost exploded in his chest.

She filled his consciousness, her lips and tongue molten in his mouth, arms wrapped around his neck, hands dragging at his hair, her body pressed so close to his he wasn't sure where she stopped and he began.

Just when he thought he'd die of ecstasy, she peeled herself away from him and staggered back a step. They stared at each other in dazed confusion and were about to launch themselves into another tangle of arms and legs, when they were interrupted by a calm, soothing voice.

"Lady Guinevere. Lord Lorenzo. May I suggest that you save these emotions for a more appropriate place?" Merlin eyes twinkled with amusement as he approached the panting, disheveled pair.

Gwen whipped around to face him, eyes wild with the power that had allowed her to tame the magical maelstrom before throwing her into a sexual frenzy.

The eldest *Old One* waved the vibrating lines of power into submission with a carefully constructed sigil, and Gwen collapsed into Mei's arms. A few steps away, Dylan calmed Renzo's aura with the same sigil.

"That must have been some ride." Dylan released his hold on Renzo and watched as the younger *Old One* took a deep breath and fought to bring him into focus.

"It's a good thing you formed the link with us before you left the apartment." His eyes twinkled as Renzo's face suffused with color. "Then again, maybe you'd prefer that we hadn't interrupted this particular scene? Not the kind of danger you were expecting when you asked us along as guards?" Dylan chuckled at his own wit.

"Knock it off. You know perfectly well I wasn't planning to seduce her on this mountain." Renzo's voice was little more than a growl. The calming sigil had done its work, but he was still on a razor's edge of animal instinct. He looked around as Merlin approached. "Is Gwen all right?"

Merlin had the good grace not to smile. "She's fine. She'll be ready to retrieve the sign in another moment or two." He studied Renzo's face with a thoughtful expression. "Did anything unusual happen this morning? Can you think of any reason she would have had that much difficulty reigning in her power?"

Renzo considered the question carefully. He wasn't anxious to reveal too much, but he didn't want to omit anything that might help Merlin untangle this particular knot. "Give me some time to think about that one. Right now, let's find the sign and get Gwen to the safety of the glade. Then we can take our time considering all the ramifications."

Merlin nodded and glanced at Gwen and Mei. "Are you ready to proceed, Lady Guinevere?"

Gwen stood up, swept her hair from her face and nodded once, regally. She was poised and under control, but with a wan delicacy that made Renzo think she would shatter if anyone touched her. His fingers itched to hold that fiery passion once again, but he stood still, maintaining a safe distance between them.

Merlin snapped his fingers and his staff appeared in his hand. "To our stations then."

The *Old One* guard ranged itself around Gwen. Merlin stood to the north, facing Gwen he measured the distance between them and then turned to face outward. Dylan repeated his action at the south compass point. Mei took the east position, and Renzo guarded her to the west. Each *Old One* held a staff, and at Merlin's signal, they raised them in unison.

Instantly, Gwen was encompassed in a shield of magical energy. Alone for all practical purposes, with nothing to interfere in the final phase of her search. She was mortified by her earlier behavior, but knew she was capable of putting that aside and fulfilling her obligation to High Magic.

Taking a calming breath, Gwen sought for the golden glow which had drawn her out of the maelstrom.

Until that moment, she had been too consumed by her passion and subsequent embarrassment to notice her surroundings. Now she realized she was standing in a dense jungle. The rain forest on the slope of Kilimanjaro was so thick with vegetation that she needed a moment to locate the subtle shimmer of the sign.

There.

Embedded in the trunk of a large sycamore tree, a common specimen in the rain forests of this region. She walked steadily to the tree, stretched out her hand, and released the sign from the surrounding wood as easily as she might have plucked an apple from an overhanging branch.

When the sign was safely on her bracelet, she called to her friends, "I have it. We can leave now."

As soon as he heard her words, Merlin adjusted the magic fields that held the canopy of protection in place and transported them all to the safety of the overworld glade.

CHAPTER 15

The moment his feet hit the ground in the overworld glade, Renzo ran to Gwen's side. He barely had time to notice the fragile expression in her eyes or her brittle smile before he swept her into his arms. He closed his eyes as he held her tightly against his chest. No sound escaped his lips as his mind skimmed the surface of the barrier she had erected in her embarrassment.

The feather touch was enough.

She dropped her guard, allowing him access to her thoughts.

Everything's all right, he whispered into her mind, imbuing his thoughts with soothing calm. *We'll figure out what happened. It was just a fluke. See... I'm holding you, and nothing horrible is happening.*

Gwen's breathing relaxed. The unnatural rigidity of her body dissipated. She nestled deeper into his arms, her cheek resting comfortably against his chest. He could almost hear a soft bubble of laughter in her answer.

You're right. I'm safe, and this is very nice... but we're not alone. She wriggled free as she sent that last thought to him.

Reluctantly, he released her.

Mei, Merlin and Dylan stood a few paces away, quietly talking among themselves. They looked up as Renzo and Gwen approached, hand-in-hand.

Merlin spoke first. "Congratulations, milady. You now have possession of four of the seven signs. Considering the forces arrayed against you, that is a commendable feat."

"Thank you, Lord Merlin, for your praise as well as your assistance."

She paused, bit her lip, and then looked him squarely in the eye. "Forgive me, if this is impertinent, but," she stopped again, then blurted out, "do you think we could drop the *Lord* and *Lady* stuff? I mean, if it's not too disrespectful."

Her cheeks flamed scarlet as she stumbled into silence.

Merlin blinked his bird-of-prey eyes twice in surprise, then laughed softly. "Of course, Gwen. We do tend to wear our formality like a shield."

He chuckled again, and the other Old Ones replaced their momentarily wary expressions with relieved smiles.

"We really have no need of shields in this particular group. So, down to business." He motioned with his staff, conjuring five comfortable chairs, and gestured for the group to be seated. "Tell me about your morning, Gwen. You needn't go into intimate details, but tell me about anything that was unusual."

Gwen's cheeks, which had been in the process of returning to their normal color, went a little rosy again, but she controlled her emotions and answered him honestly.

"I think the main difference was that I woke up rested. My nights have been, well, haunted, since the attack. But last night was different. I slept soundly— no nightmares— and woke up feeling great. I figured it had something to do with Lughnasadh."

She paused to gather her thoughts, and Renzo took up the narrative.

"I've been aware that she hasn't been sleeping. In fact, this was the first morning I've been up before her. I took it as a good sign, especially when she was in such a happy mood when she did make it to the kitchen."

Merlin nodded thoughtfully. "Yes, that could certainly be a reflection of Lughnasadh's heightened magic. What else?"

Realization hit Gwen like a physical blow. "My senses. They're functioning normally again." She noticed the startled looks on the other's faces, but focused her attention on Merlin's tawny eyes as she hastened to explain.

"This morning my senses were so acute it was almost painful. Everything was overwhelming to me. I had my back to Renzo, because looking at him was too much. Everything was too much." She stopped, closed her eyes and tried to remember the sensation. "When he touched me, put his arms around me... it was like everything just exploded out of control."

Her eyes flew open. "I had to fight to hold the lines of power. I've never had to fight to control a search before. I've always just let it roll over me, take me where I needed to go."

Dylan skewered Renzo with his eyes. "Were you aware of any of this?"

"Not until I put my arms around her and we kicked into hyperdrive. But then, I've never been in physical contact with her during a search. I had no basis for comparison." He rubbed his hands over his face. "It certainly wasn't the serene flight I've witnessed on other High Days." And he definitely didn't want to discuss the landing... that was a treasured memory to be savored when he was alone.

"This puts an entirely different light on things." Merlin glanced around the circle of *Old Ones*. "Renzo, as soon as you get back, check your immediate vicinity for fissures. A newly opening crack could account for Gwen's acute sensory perceptions as well as her extreme difficulty with nightmares. Yes, yes, I know." He held up a hand to ward off Mei's objections. "A certain amount of psychic distress is to be expected after her trauma... but she should be able to get at least *some* undisturbed sleep. She is a magical being after all."

"A fissure? What's a fissure?" Gwen looked at Merlin, eyes wide with confusion. "What would a geologic fault have to do with my sensory overload? Or my sleep?"

"The fissures he's talking about aren't geologic," Dylan answered. "They're disruptions in the lines of magical power. We don't really understand them. The current theory is that they're openings to a parallel reality."

Mei spoke for the first time, her voice light and cool after the low masculine rumble. "The important thing is that they pollute the lines of power, making them unpredictable and difficult to control. It's possible that the larger fissures even warp the mind of the *Old One* trying to use the lines."

She shrugged her shoulders delicately. "We like to think that's what happened to Lilith. It's easier than believing she would consciously choose to become the filthy, evil being that she has."

"Why wasn't I warned about them, if they're potentially dangerous?" Gwen's eyes snapped, though she tried to keep the irritation out of her voice.

"That would be my fault," Dylan admitted wearily. "It's obviously been too long since I last trained a fledgling *Old One*. I was so concerned with making sure you could deal with Lilith, I forgot about the fissures. I haven't been near one in several centuries. They're not nearly rare enough, but they're not exactly common-place either."

"I'm sorry, Dylan. I didn't mean to make that an accusation." Gwen sighed and stood up. "It's been a stressful morning, and I still have a full day of classes ahead of me."

Dylan's face darkened. "Speaking of classes, stay as far away from Dr. Whittier as you can. Make sure you're never alone with that man."

"Excuse me?" The sudden change of topic caused Gwen to collapse back into her chair. "What does he have to do with anything?"

"Nothing on his own. Unfortunately, he's under Lilith's influence." Dylan turned his attention from Gwen to Merlin and gave the *Old One* a brief rundown on the irascible professor. "So," he finished, "I used my university credentials to arrange a meeting with him. He's definitely under Lilith's control. I tried a few sigils to see if I could release him— or at least block her from further interference— but it was useless. He's firmly ensorcelled." Dylan returned his gaze to Gwen. "Be very careful in his presence."

Gwen swallowed hard and nodded her agreement. "I will. Thank you for taking me seriously and checking him out."

"Of course. I've never known you to be overly dramatic. You said there was a problem, so I knew I needed to meet him. I'm very sorry for the man. I hope we can free him before he's perma-nently damaged."

Gwen nodded as understanding flooded her soul: Dr. Whittier was an innocent. He needed her protection. Unfortunately, she didn't have any idea how to break his enchantment. But she could stay out of his way. Maybe if she wasn't in any of his courses, Lilith would lose interest in him.

Yeah, right.

And the cat will release the mouse if it simply refuses to run.

CHAPTER 16

*D*uring the last two weeks of the summer session, Gwen made a determined effort to remain silent in Dr. Whittier's class. When required to speak, she carefully avoided making eye contact with him. The extent of Lilith's control wasn't clear, but Dylan and Renzo both felt it might intensify if Gwen confronted Whittier directly. Outside of his classroom, staying out of his way was a breeze; Gwen simply barricaded herself in her apartment and got on with the business of finishing the term.

Meanwhile, Renzo made a thorough search of the area surrounding Gwen's apartment for fissures and warps in the magical power lines. Merlin's supposition proved correct. A fissure had opened a few blocks away. Renzo hadn't felt it at Lughnasadh simply because he hadn't been using magic. As soon as he found it, he conferred with Kunto and Omar. Both of those *Old Ones* lived near existing fissures and had developed warding sigils to diminish their effects.

"We haven't found a way to heal the rifts," Kunto told Renzo, "but with the wards in place, I've been able to use my magic with no backlash. I do have to exert a stronger control near the fissure, but I've found that's actually a bonus." His wicked grin and cunning gaze reminded Renzo of a powerful jungle cat. "I'm more disciplined, and therefore more powerful, when I'm away from its influence. Truly, it's not a bad trade off."

After conferring with the his *Old One* colleagues, Renzo felt far more at ease with the situation. He taught Gwen the warding sigils, and the two of them were diligent about their use.

With the wards in place, Gwen was able to sleep comfortably most nights, and her magic was again firmly under her control.

When her last exam ended in mid-August, Renzo breathed a sigh of relief. Gwen now had six weeks before classes resumed at the end of September. Six weeks when she wouldn't be subjected to Whittier's neurotic insults. Hopefully she'd be able to avoid his classes next term.

Of course, they knew Whittier was in Lilith's camp. If Gwen stayed too far away from him, Lilith might decide she needed another operative. Maybe it would be better for Gwen to take one of Whittier's classes, just to keep Lilith mollified. After all, a known evil was easier to guard against.

"Yoo-hoo. Earth to Renzo."

Gwen's voice penetrated his worry-absorbed thoughts and he focused on her sweet face.

"Where were you? The term is over. It's time to relax." Gwen twirled around him on the sidewalk, grabbed his hand and laughed at the strained expression on his face.

She leaned toward him conspiratorially. "Don't worry. I haven't forgotten about Lilith. But term is over. I have six weeks of freedom from course work, and five weeks before Alban Elued. We've earned a break. Let's plan a vacation."

Renzo smiled as she tugged on his hand, leading him to the apartment.

"You're absolutely right. Why don't you call the management company and see if there are any openings at your condo?" He stopped and pulled her into his arms. "We could always give someone a nudge if it's fully booked. You know, give them a sudden desire to visit the Grand Canyon instead of the Oregon Coast."

Gwen laughed, gave him a quick squeeze around the waist and pulled free of his embrace. "We'll do nothing of the kind. We need to learn to schedule our vacations in advance like everyone else. I will call the manager, though. A trip to the coast sounds like heaven. Maybe I'll reserve the last two weeks of August as owner's time from now on. What do you think? Should I claim it for the Christmas and New Year's holidays as well?"

"Go for it. It'll be a great place to spend some dark and stormy nights. Who knows what might happen in front of a roaring fire..."

Their playful banter died as he saw Gwen recognize the desire beneath his words.

The world stopped.

Renzo and Gwen stood, gazes locked, rooted in the moment. They might have stood there forever— unable to look away, unwilling to speak— except for Renzo's peripheral awareness that someone, somewhere, was calling Gwen's name.

"Gwen. Guinevere Vaughan." The voice came nearer. "Gwen, snap out of it." The voice was right next to them. "What on earth are you staring at?"

～

Gwen emerged from her Renzo-induced fog to find Angela, a fellow graduate student, staring at her with open-mouthed curiosity.

"I'm sorry. Did you say something?" With difficulty, Gwen managed to avoid falling back under Renzo's spell long enough to acknowledge Angela's existence.

"I've only been yelling at you for an entire block. What's up? Are you okay?"

"I'm fine. Just a mild case of post-summer-session stress." Gwen managed to slip a sidelong glance in Renzo's direction. His eyes were as wide as her own, and she had the satisfaction of seeing chagrin wash over his face as he realized her predicament.

He'd forgotten to remove the *I'm not here* sigil after her last exam. As far as Angela knew, Gwen had been standing there mesmerized by the tree which stood a few paces behind Renzo.

Gwen's attention was drawn back to the immediate situation as Angela grabbed her arm and began to walk her toward the student union. "You obviously need a cup of coffee to snap you out of whatever haze you're in. Come on. We'll grab a bite and compare notes on our finals."

With a helpless glance at Renzo, Gwen allowed herself to be propelled down the sidewalk by the determined young woman.

CHAPTER 17

"*D*o come, dear," Mrs. Carson breathed into her cell phone. "I know Rachel won't sit still without you, and she's been working much too hard the last few weeks. I'm sure you could do with some down time since you've just finished your first term in grad school. And I *know* Rachel needs it. I'll fix lunch, and then leave you two alone. You can talk, read, swim or just doze in the sun. Whatever you like, just so long as neither of you talks about anything even vaguely work-related."

The pleading note in her voice made Gwen a little uneasy. Mrs. Carson was usually so upbeat and positive.

"Of course, I'll come." Gwen said enthusiastically. It never hurt to lay it on a little thick with Rachel's mom. "How could I resist lazing by the pool on a summer day? What time, and what can I bring?"

Mrs. Carson's laugh skittered across Gwen's nerves. How did she manage to sound relieved and nervous at the same time?

"Fabulous, dear. Come around noon, and you needn't bring a thing— just your swimsuit and a book. This day is on me."

The moment Gwen stepped through the front door of the Carson's stately Georgian home, she knew something was wrong. Elizabeth Carson, a woman at ease in any social situation, was visibly nervous. Her hand trembled as she took Gwen's arm and guided her into the house. Her eyes slid quickly past Gwen's face in an obvious effort not to connect. Elizabeth's laughter was too quick and too high to indicate true enjoyment of Gwen's casual banter.

What was wrong?

Lilith!

Could Lilith be threatening the Carson's in some way? Was Gwen walking into a carefully baited trap? Her hands ached at the thought and she wished she hadn't insisted that Renzo give her some space today. What if this was the one place she truly needed his protection?

Taking a deep breath, she forced herself to be calm. If she needed Renzo, she'd call him. She readied the sigil for mindspeech as a precaution. She refused to be paranoid, but she wasn't about to be caught off-guard again either.

Preparations made, her shallow breathing regulated, and she followed Elizabeth Carson calmly into the great room.

"Rachel, look who's here." Elizabeth's attempt to sound bright and cheerful sounded strained to Gwen's ears but the moment she saw her friend, she understood the source of Mrs. Carson's unease.

Rachel looked like hell.

"You girls have a nice chat. I'll call you when lunch is on the table."

Gwen doubted that Elizabeth Carson had ever made a swifter retreat from an uncomfortable social obligation.

Turning her attention from mother to daughter, Gwen studied her friend. Rachel's normally shiny blonde hair was dull and tangled. Her eyes were puffy. Had she been crying? If so, it had been a serious storm, and she hadn't made any attempt to repair the damage with cosmetics. When she raised her eyes to Gwen's, the normal sparkle was missing. Pain throbbed in her dull blue gaze, and Gwen's conscience flared.

How could she not have known her friend was so distraught?

"Rachel. What's wrong?" Gwen ran across the intervening distance and wrapped Rachel in a protective hug. "What's happened? Is your dad ill?"

Gwen couldn't imagine anything, short of a death in the family, that would make her friend abandon her grooming like this. Even her clothing screamed *distress*. In the months since they'd found each other again, Gwen had never seen Rachel like this. She was wearing sweats… and stained ones at that.

"David." Rachel uttered the single word as if it explained the world. She took a deep breath and let it out with a shuddering sigh. "He doesn't want me anymore."

Gwen held Rachel at arms' length and peered into her eyes. Rachel's control was about to break, and when it did a flood would wash over them both. Quickly Gwen eased Rachel onto the couch and sat down beside her, being careful not to break the physical contact that seemed to be the only thing holding her friend together.

"Tell me everything," she commanded.

Rachel's eyes slipped past her to the door where her mother had recently vanished.

"Your mom will hold lunch for us," she said, correctly interpreting the glance. "What happened? Why didn't you call me?"

Rachel gave her a wan smile that came nowhere near her eyes. "You've been through so much recently. I didn't want to add to your pain. Mom didn't tell me she'd asked you here. She just came by my apartment this morning and bullied me until I dressed and came home with her."

A sad little laugh escaped her lips. "She wouldn't even let me drive my own car. Said I was a menace to society in my present state."

Gwen's face suffused with color. Shame stabbed her heart and blazed in her blood. How could she have been so self-absorbed that she'd failed to see or even talk to Rachel for nearly two weeks? A quick mental calculation confirmed that they hadn't been in contact since the four of them had celebrated the finding of the Lughnasadh sign.

The four of them.

She couldn't imagine that David was gone.

Not only did he belong with Rachel, but the two of them belonged with her and Renzo.

Renzo...

Okay, so she wasn't totally self-absorbed. She was also Renzo-absorbed.

That had to change. Gwen had to remember that he wasn't her entire universe. She also had friends and family she cared deeply for, and she'd obviously been failing in that care.

But she was being self-absorbed again. This wasn't about her. This was about Rachel. And David.

Gwen studied Rachel's red-rimmed, puffy eyes and made a decision. "I'd like you to tell me everything; if you're willing. But right now, you need food. Do you want me to come upstairs with you while you wash your face and brush your hair?"

"Are you insinuating I need help with my grooming?" Rachel's smile finally reached her eyes. Momentarily.

"Well, duh. Have you looked at yourself recently?" Gwen hugged her tightly for a second, then stood up. "Come on. You'll feel better if you spruce up a bit. And you won't scare your mom as much either."

Rachel's eyes widened. "What?"

"Seriously, she was so on edge that I was ready to run for cover. I was half convinced Lilith was waiting for me in here."

"Oh. It hadn't occurred to me that I might be scaring her." Rachel stood up, looked down at her grimy sweats and then back to Gwen. "You go help Mom. There's still some clothes in my old bedroom. I'll make myself presentable."

She reached for Gwen's hand and squeezed it tightly. "Thanks. A true friend tells the truth— even when it's uncomfortable. We'll talk after lunch."

Mrs. Carson heaved a sigh of relief when Rachel appeared in the dining room with her face freshly scrubbed, wearing a pair of denim shorts and a pink tank top.

Lunch was pleasant. The company easy, if not fully relaxed. The food— ripe red tomatoes hollowed out and filled with tuna salad, a selection of crisp, gourmet crackers, seedless green grapes, and iced tea— was filling and delicious.

Obviously relieved by Rachel's improved attitude and appearance, Elizabeth Carson shooed the girls off to the pool when they finished eating. "You two run along and bask. I don't need any help clearing this tiny mess. I'll be in the library reading if you need anything." Her eyes lingered lovingly on Rachel. "Shoo... you're keeping me from an absolutely fascinating novel."

Rachel laughed, hugged her mom and led Gwen to the backyard pool. Before settling in, she grabbed a pair of sunglasses from a patio table and raided the poolside cooler for a couple of diet colas. Handing Gwen a cola, and looking much more like herself, blonde hair neatly tucked into a scrunchie on top of her head, Rachel reclined on a outdoor lounge chair and prepared to soak up a little late summer sun.

After settling into her own lounge, Gwen studied her friend's profile. "Do you want to talk about it?"

"Not really, but I will." Rachel reached up and pushed the sunglasses to the top of her head. She turned to face Gwen. "It happened last Sunday night. He took me out to a really nice restaurant. Everything was perfect. Candles on the table, flowers, wine, the whole nine yards. I was sure he was going to pop the question. I was so excited I could hardly sit still. I mean, I'm not sure I'm ready for marriage, but at the same time, I know he's the one. I love him. I thought he loved me." Her monologue shuddered to a halt.

Gwen sat quietly, waiting to see if she would continue.

After a minute, Rachel reached for her can of diet cola, took a swallow, and continued her narration. "Well, I was kind of right. He did ask me a question. Just not the right one." She paused again and pulled her sunglasses back down, hiding her eyes.

"He asked me to move in with him." Her voice was flat, clearly demonstrating the depth of her disappointment.

"What did you say?" Gwen asked quietly.

Rachel flashed her a wry smile. "I handled it very badly. I'd been so sure it was going to be something else. I said all the wrong things." She leaned her head back against the lounge chair with a sigh. "I told him I loved him, that I wanted to make a life with him. I came right out and said I wanted to marry him... not play house with him."

"Oh, my." Gwen paused, at a momentary loss for words. "I take it he didn't appreciate that fine distinction."

It wasn't a question. It was a statement of fact.

"No. He told me to grow up. That just because my best friend lived in a fairy tale didn't mean I could afford to." She paused again to sip her cola. The hand holding the can trembled.

"He probably would have said more, but I didn't wait to find out. I ran to the ladies room and cried myself silly. When I finally came out, the Maitre 'D called a cab for me. I left without checking to see if he was still there. I haven't heard from him since."

Gwen sighed. "I'm so sorry, honey. Do you want me to talk to him?"

Rachel shook her head. "It wouldn't do any good. I've said the L-word and the M-word. We can't go back to being friends. I don't want to move in with him. He doesn't want to marry me. I don't see much room for negotiation."

Rachel lapsed into silence, and Gwen observed a single tear slide down her cheek.

Gwen stared into the distance, at a loss as to how to help her friend. She glanced at the still water of the pool and came to a decision.

"You need a change of scenery. Ask your dad for a few days off and come out to the coast with me. My parents left me a condo at Cannon Beach and I've managed to wangle the management company out of a spur of the moment week."

Rachel sat up a little straighter in her chair, then slumped again. "Isn't Renzo going with you?"

"Well, yes. It took an act of Congress to get him to let me come here alone today. He certainly won't let me get that far away from his protective custody. But it's a two bedroom condo. He can have one room; you and I can share the other. I'll tell him to guard us from a distance. He won't mind."

"Yeah, right. You can't tell me that man doesn't have designs on your body. He's probably really looking forward to whisking you away to the coast." She sighed heavily. "I've screwed up my own love life. I'm not anxious to do yours in as well."

"Rachel, look at me. Renzo and I will work out our own relationship. I definitely have feelings for him, and I know he cares for me. But we're not lovers. If I want you to come to the coast with me for a few days, he'll just have to deal."

"Well... let me see what Dad says before we make any firm plans." She reached for Gwen's hand. "I'll talk to Dad, and you talk to Renzo. Then we'll play it by ear. I'd love to go, but I really don't want to get in your way."

"Deal. I'll call you in the morning, and we'll see what's up."

CHAPTER 18

*T*he week at the coast was wonderful. Gwen watched happily as color bloomed in Rachel's cheeks once more. They took early morning walks through the surf that fringed the wide white beach. Enjoyed drives along the coast highway and picnicked at several of the myriad road side beach parks.

One of Gwen's personal favorites was Strawberry Hill. She loved climbing down the windswept hill onto the rocks that jutted stolidly into the ocean. It was almost like a return to childhood. Scrambling around on those rocky crags, exploring tidal pools, and spying on harbor seals basking serenely, secure in the knowledge that their rocks were cut off from human incursion by wide circles of sea.

Renzo, of course, accompanied them everywhere they went. For Rachel's peace of mind, he often used the *I'm not here* sigil, allowing her the illusion of privacy as she healed. Frequently, Rachel succumbed to the temptation to nap in the afternoon sun. When that happened, Renzo and Gwen enjoyed the blissful magic that was uniquely their own.

On their last day at Cannon Beach, the three friends sat on their deck watching the breakers roll in as they ate a lazy breakfast of warm apple fritters, coffee, and summer berries. Without warning, Gwen felt herself being pulled into her gelatinous search bubble.

Rachel, sitting across the table from her, cried out and reached for Gwen's hand.

"Gwen? What's wrong?" The color drained from Rachel's face as she watched the trance develop.

Gwen's eyes lost their focus, her face reflected a fierce intensity which frightened her friend. The unnatural rigidity of her spine reflected a supernatural control of her physical body.

"Don't touch her, Rachel." Renzo's voice was quiet, but there was no mistaking the tone of command. "She's seeking. More than likely the next sign clue has called her." He smiled into Rachel's panicked eyes. "Trust me. She's fine. This is part of her gift."

Those last words had barely cleared his lips when Gwen snapped back to consciousness. Her body lost its tension and her eyes cleared. She tossed them a radiant smile. "Come on. We're hiking down to Haystack Rock. There's a sand dollar there with my name on it."

Gwen sprinted the last few yards with Rachel at her side. "This is actually the second time you've been with me when I found a clue. Remember my sudden desire for a stone from the Willamette?"

Rachel stopped where she was and stared open-mouthed. "You mean that little rock was important?" She had to put some force behind her words to make them heard over the pounding surf.

Gwen flashed her a grin and ran unerringly to a select spot at the base of the massive pillar of basalt. Once there, she bent and quickly pocketed a nondescript sand dollar. Joining Rachel again, she threw an arm around her shoulders and edged her toward the condo.

"Let's get back to Renzo and see if this clue is ready to reveal itself."

RENZO RESTED NONCHALANTLY on the balcony and watched the young women's progress toward the huge basalt sea stack. When he felt himself in danger of losing sight of them, he extended his senses and wrapped the lines of magic firmly around the sigil he sketched in the air. Instantly his vision heightened and he continued his silent guardianship. He breathed a sigh of relief as Gwen pocket the small white circle and made her way back toward the safety of his arms.

CHAPTER 19

*T*he sand dollar refused to divulge its secrets, so Gwen, Rachel, and Renzo returned to Portland, and Gwen went to work at the museum. She'd let her work there slide while she completed the summer term at PSU and took her week at the coast. Now it was time to buckle down and catch up.

Rachel and David's split caused some awkwardness for Gwen. Rachel was part of her personal life, while David belonged to her professional life. She'd thought when they'd been made privy to her *Old One* life that she was past compartmentalizing her existence, but here she was again... forced to keep competing elements apart.

But her quest overrode her friends' emotional upheaval.

Gwen glanced at David as he leaned against her cubicle wall, observing her efforts to translate an Aztec text. "Will you come over this evening and help me decipher my next clue? Alban Elued begins at dusk tomorrow. I'm hoping the clue will allow me twenty-four hours to figure out its meaning."

"I'd love to help." He paused, eyes scanning the room. The color in his face rose slightly as he looked everywhere except at Gwen. "Will Rachel be there?"

Gwen swallowed the impatience that threatened to erupt in scathing words. Instead, she answered with determined calmness. "Yes, of course, she will. The four of us are a team." She paused, then commanded, "David. Look at me."

When he finally focused on her, she continued, "I can remove your memory of the arcane, if you'd rather not continue working with us."

She wasn't threatening him.

She was offering him a way out

David scrubbed a hand across his face and knelt beside her chair. "No. I agreed to help, and I want to continue. I just never expected things to get weird between Rachel and me." He took a deep breath and held it for a moment. After he expelled it, he asked, "What time do you want me there?"

"Come over as soon after work as you can manage. We'll provide the pizza and beer." She gave him a quick grin. "If the sand dollar doesn't cooperate, it'll be a very short meeting."

GWEN DIDN'T TRY to make dinner a social event. David and Rachel were much too tense to enjoy each other's company, so they simply plopped pizza slices onto plates, grabbed cans of beer and made themselves comfortable in the living room. When everyone was seated, Renzo produced a white board. The sand dollar sat on the coffee table in plain sight.

Gwen enjoyed a slice of pizza, relishing the tangy red sauce, the pepperoni, and the excellent blend of cheeses. When only a bite of crust remained, she set her plate aside and reached for the sand dollar.

"Let's see if this is ready to give up its clue."

"How do you know it has one to give up?" Rachel asked eyeing the white disk. "It looks like an ordinary sand dollar to me. Are you sure you picked up the right one?"

Gwen snorted. "It's the right one. Trust me. I could feel the sigil pulling me even before I picked it up just now. It's just a matter of timing." She fell silent as she clasped the sand dollar in her two hands. Closing her eyes, she concentrated on the sigil only she knew was there. Opening her eyes, she held the sand dollar out for their inspection.

Renzo saw the sigil glowing deep within the shell. He watched in fascination as it shimmered to the surface. "Can you two see it?" he asked, his voice hushed.

"See what?" David stared blankly at the simple shell lying on Gwen's upturned palm. He glanced up as Gwen chortled.

"Well, I guess that answers your question, Renzo." Merriment bubbled from her lips. "Sorry, David. I'm not laughing at you. The whole situation just struck me as funny."

"So, is the clue ready or not?" Rachel asked sharply, throwing an angry glance at David.

"It's ready. Rachel, would you write it on the board, please?" Gwen waited while Rachel found a marker and moved to the white board. When all was in readiness, she touched the sigil glowing on the surface of the sand dollar.

Words swam lazily through her mind, drifting just out of reach until a complete phrase formed, then it blazed just long enough for her to call it out to Rachel... then the words separated and eddied away, while the next line drifted together, to blaze and then separate. This continued until all eight lines were captured in Rachel's neat block letters on the white board.

> Once again on the wheel a balance is found;
> Light and Dark, Good and Evil; rivals unbound.
> Soon Light will diminish and Darkness will grow,
> But Light of the Water is equal in trow
>
> The fifth sign of seven is sustained in the fall,
> Water in abundance flows free o'er the wall.
> "I am the highest. I am proud. I am free."
> Cries the mighty Carrao on its way to the sea.

"Cool," said David, as Rachel moved away from the board to sit next to Gwen on the couch. "Where's this wheel that's balanced? Somehow, I doubt that's a reference to balancing the wheels on your car."

"Taken in context, I'd say it's a reference to the wheel of the year." Renzo sat back, placing his arm on the back of the couch— just above Gwen's shoulders. "That's an ancient term for calendar."

"In that case, *balance* would refer to the equinox, when the hours of light and dark are equal." Rachel looked to Gwen for confirmation. "So *once again* must refer to the second equinox of the year; the autumnal equinox."

"That makes sense," David added, "from that point on the days get shorter, which is probably what that third line is referring to." He studied the rhyme again. "What does *light of the water* have to do with anything?"

"Another ancient reference. It's the literal translation of Alban Elued. The old name for the autumnal equinox." Renzo turned away from the board to look at Gwen. "Once again, we seem to have the proper clue for the season."

Gwen grimaced as she glanced back to the rhyme. "Have you noticed how idiot proof these clues are? I mean, you can't access the blasted thing until the appointed time, and then they spend the first few lines confirming that you've got the right High Day."

Once again, Rachel brought the group back into focus, saying, "Well, I'm happy to know we're on the right track. What do you think the rest of it means?"

"Fifth sign of seven. Yeah, yeah, we know, we're doing it in the right order. But *sustained in the fall*?" David looked at each of them in turn. "It's September twentieth. Is it officially Fall yet?"

"It will be tomorrow." Rachel tried not to meet his gaze as she answered. "The solstices and equinoxes mark the change of seasons. So, autumn begins with the autumnal equinox."

"Correct. But I don't think fall is a reference to season here." Renzo stood up and walked to the window and back, frowning in concentration as he paced. He turned back to study the board. "Look at the next line, which is part of the same sentence, it's all about water."

"Yes," Gwen cried. "Water flowing over a wall. The water would be falling. Oh," she gasped and slapped her forehead with the heel of her hand. "A waterfall. We're looking for a waterfall."

"Good job, Gwen." Rachel beamed at her friend.

David flushed and looked away from his former girlfriend. Gwen wondered if he could be having second thoughts. The pair had barely glanced at each other all evening.

But Rachel didn't seem bothered by any remorse as she followed up on Gwen's insight. "Do you think we can ignore *proud* and *free*, and just concentrate on *highest*? Or is there some unwritten rule that every single word is significant?"

Gwen nodded, enjoying the exchange of ideas, but wishing their little team was still as cohesive as it had been a month ago. Shaking off the thought of what might have been, she said, "Hey, it's our quest. We can approach the clues any way we want. What are you thinking?"

Rachel hesitated a moment before blurting out her idea. "What if *the mighty Carrao* is a river, and we're looking for the highest waterfall along its route? Would that fit the sense of the thing?"

"I think that's a masterful piece of reasoning." Renzo came back from the kitchen with another slice of pizza. "We just need to check it out. Got an atlas, Gwen?"

"Hrmph." David snorted. "Why do it the hard way when there's a computer on the desk. You don't mind do you, Gwen?" He sat down, typing as he asked the question.

"Nope. You'll notice I already had it on this time." She laughed, delighted with the progress they were making. She glanced from David, sitting at the keyboard, fingers flying, to Rachel, standing at the kitchen table picking olives off her pizza. If only there was a way to heal the rift between them...

Her thoughts were interrupted by David's shout of triumph. "Way to go Rachel. You nailed it. Not only does the Carrao have a big waterfall," he paused dramatically, "it has the highest waterfall in the world. Angel Falls. Your sign is in Venezuela, Gwen. At Angel Falls."

CHAPTER 20

This time the *Old Ones* met in advance. At dawn on Alban Elued Merlin, Mei and Dylan materialized in Gwen's kitchen.

"Welcome to my home. May I offer you something to eat before we begin?" Gwen stood with a platter of warm cinnamon rolls in one hand and a pot of coffee in the other. The scent of the rolls and coffee combined to underscore her words with comfortable hospitality.

"Thank you, Gwen. What a delightful welcome." Merlin took a roll and sat companionably at her table. The other *Old Ones* followed his example with eager rapidity. As they made themselves at home, Gwen distributed copies of the latest clue.

"You've done a good job with the wards." Dylan moved to join Renzo as the younger man sauntered into the room. "I hardly feel the fissure's influence at all."

"Thanks. We've been diligent with our work on that front." Renzo glanced toward Gwen. "I know she's not anxious to repeat the circumstances of that last search." He gave Dylan a conspiratorial wink and lowered his voice. "Not that I had any complaints."

Dylan guffawed, causing the rest of the group to turn and stare at him. "Sorry. Didn't mean to interrupt." He and Renzo assumed innocent expressions and joined the others at the table. "What's our game plan?"

Gwen eyed the two men suspiciously before answering. "We're headed to Angel Falls in Venezuela. I don't see any reason not to begin my search right now, since we're all together. Do the rest of you want to go on ahead?"

"No. I think we should all stay in contact." Merlin scanned their faces as he spoke. "Renzo, you maintain a link with Gwen. The rest of us will piggy-back on your connection." Merlin fell silent as his eyes skimmed the wording of the clue. "It occurs to me that we may not be able to take up the traditional compass points in our warding this time. If the sign is truly suspended in the waters of the falls, the best we'll be able to accomplish will be a semicircular umbrella of protection." He lapsed into silence again, eyes slightly unfocused as he envisioned a possible scenario.

"Perhaps we should cocoon Gwen in a shield here." Mei spoke quietly, weighing each word. "She could carry that shielding with her as she quests, and when we arrived, we would be able to augment its power."

"Good thought, Mei." Dylan nodded his agreement, excitement telegraphing from him to his companions. "Do you think we could use High Magic's protective charm as a base for our sigil? Gwen carries that with her wherever she goes, and it's already designed to envelope her in a protective shield."

"Yes," Renzo agreed. "Why haven't I thought of that before? We can amplify High Magic's charm. Beef it up so that it protects her from mortal intervention as well as magical."

Merlin nodded. "Yes. That will work for this situation." He held up a cautionary hand. "But don't try to use it on a daily basis, Renzo. It would prevent her from normal interaction with mortals. You'd spend all your time altering their memories and healing their hurts." His eyes twinkled as Renzo's face reddened.

"Busted. I was already trying to figure out how to do just that."

"Okay then." Gwen's exuberant voice demanded their attention. "Do what you need to do, but let's get this show on the road. I want this next sign safely on my bracelet as soon as possible."

The process didn't take long. Before she knew it, Gwen stood on a ledge about a thousand feet up the wall of Auyan Tepui— the tabletop mountain over which the Carrao River plunged in its headlong race to the sea. Gwen's ledge being too small to support them, her honor guard watched nervously from an outcropping across and several hundred feet below.

Gwen glowed with an ethereal blue light, the physical manifestation of the boost to her protective charm, but that didn't concern her. Her senses were deluged by the roar of the immense waterfall as it plummeted to the jungle below. She closed her eyes, suspended in time and space, alone in a mist of water.

The flood roared; its spray drenched her clothes and skin, but her mind's eye focused on the golden glow that danced within the descending water. Opening her eyes to a blue-gray world, and with no thought to the surety of her footing, Gwen stepped forward, plunging her hand into the race of water.

Yes!

She had it! The sign solidified in her hand as she withdrew her fist from the rushing, roaring deluge.

Raising her fist above her head in a triumphant gesture, Gwen turned to grin at her friends across the abyss.

Without warning, a man materialized on the ledge beside her. He grabbed for her, obviously intending to throw her off the ledge. Her protective spell flattened him against the side of the cliff before she realized he was there, let alone registered his malicious intent.

Gwen. Renzo's voice sounded urgently in her mind. *Don't touch him. Your protective sigil will throw him off the cliff. Go home. Leave him to us.*

I understand. She was surprised by the calmness of her thought. She exchanged a sorrowful glance with her would-be attacker— and vanished.

CHAPTER 21

*J*ason Whittier gazed in satisfaction at the young woman perched on his sofa. She was perfection. An aging man's dream.

Hell! *Any* man's dream!

Old enough to be fully ripe— the cotton blouse buttoned chastely to the neck couldn't hide her voluptuous curves— but young enough that he would be the first to enjoy that firm young body.

He knew he would be the first.

Young women who were aware of their sexual power didn't dress like nineteenth century librarians. Her beauty was flawless, but she was deliciously unaware of her latent sexuality. He knew he should be ashamed, taking advantage of such innocence, but all he felt was desperate arousal.

She would be his.

Tonight.

And he was going to enjoy every moment to the hilt. He smiled at his own wit. Yes, *to the hilt*, that was an accurate phrase.

Her beautiful blue eyes met his, shyly, as she accepted a flute of champagne from his hand.

Honestly, he should be whipped! Plying this woman-child with strong drink to have his way with her. His eyes sparkled and he enjoyed a moment's thrill by simply caressing her fingers.

Oh yes, this was going to be a night to remember.

Afterward, he was never sure of all the intoxicating details that led from that first glass of champagne to their naked, sweating bodies tangled on his bed. He just knew it had been the ride of his life.

Now he was fully in the moment again. His flesh pounding into her warm, soft, but excitingly firm, curves. With each penetration, he felt himself step closer to that edge of annihilation. The cliff face that would garner him the exquisite pleasure of release, while flinging him into the abyss of her awakened power. To counter that awakening, he chanted to himself, unaware that he spoke the words aloud.

"You are mine." He thrust, exulting in her answering moan. "All mine." Another deep penetration, the effort causing his eyes, and mind, to glaze. "We are sealed."

A final earth-shattering thrust and his world exploded. Stars of light quickened behind his eyelids as he exhaled in exhaustion and fell heavily on her unprotesting softness.

The sound that came from her lips froze him to the bone.

She didn't sigh with sexual contentment; didn't moan with first-time fright or pain; didn't even laugh with new-found prowess.

She screamed with unabashed triumph.

"Get off me, you pig!"

"But, my dear. That was wonderful. No need to be upset." He tried to soothe the manic sound from his ears. His eyes widened as he looked into her face and truly saw her for the first time.

"Be silent," she commanded, and he obeyed.

He had no choice. His jaw locked and his vocal chords froze.

"Get off me. *Now.*"

His body flew from hers; he hung suspended a few feet above his bed. Languidly she drew some sort of sign in the air... and his mind cleared. His thoughts took on a clarity they'd lacked for the last few months.

Laughing, she studied him as confusion and terror crowded all thoughts of sexual satisfaction from his mind. She stretched, cat-like, and stepped regally from the bed.

"Know me now, mortal. I am Lilith. Your Goddess. You may grovel at my feet."

Instantly his body slammed into the carpet, his face cocked so that her perfect toes filled his vision. "You have willingly given me power over your body. I hold your seed within myself. It binds your will to mine." She stroked his cheek with her toe, then kicked him over and levitated him until their gazes met.

"No one forced you to seduce an innocent young maiden. You made your choice— and, in so doing, handed me the keys to your soul. Such as it is." She smiled, satisfaction glinting in her eyes.

How could he have ever thought her beautiful?

CHAPTER 22

The final days of September brought the start of Gwen's first full term as a graduate student. Her pace of life quickened dramatically. She was now carrying a full schedule of classes, while still maintaining enough hours at the Museum to support herself. Her days were full, but her workload didn't stop there. When she finally made it home in the early evenings, she still faced several hours of research and study before she could finally fall into bed each night.

Renzo, continuing his careful vigilance, was both amazed at her endurance and a little frightened for her.

"You're going to burn yourself out." He watched in concern as she bolted the meal he had prepared for her. "You can't keep up this manic pace."

She laughed as she stretched, preparing to move to her desk. "Welcome to the life of a dedicated doctoral candidate." She paused in her trek to caress his cheek. "Thanks for dinner— for taking care of me, in general. It makes life so much easier."

Renzo grabbed her hand and pulled her into his lap. "Take a break," he breathed in her ear, "watch a movie with me. Relax a little."

Gwen sighed and melted into his embrace. "You really know how to tempt a girl. Maybe after I finish Whittier's paper. I should be able to hack that out in about an hour or so." She kissed him lightly on the chin, then forced herself to stand up. "Work first, play later."

He watched her settle into her desk chair before he cleared the table. He did the task by hand. Gwen was buried in her studies, he had no reason to hurry, and cleaning up after the meal gave him something to occupy his time.

Renzo was wiping down the counter tops when the doorbell rang. He jumped as the unexpected sound jangled across his nerves. Forcing himself to be calm, he extended his senses to find Jason Whittier standing outside the apartment door.

Gwen joined him before she answered the door.

"What can Whittier want with me at home?" she asked, her voice quiet and calm, but puzzled.

"I'm going to augment your charm before you open the door." He employed the sigil that had proven so efficient at Alban Elued, then used the *I'm not here* sigil on himself. "Go ahead. Open it. Just remember not to touch him."

Gwen nodded, took a calming breath, exhaled and opened her front door. "Dr. Whittier. What a surprise." She greeted the man with a smile. "Would you like to come in?"

Jason Whittier stood in the hallway and peered around her into the apartment. "Are you alone, Miss Vaughan?"

"Not a soul in sight." Gwen answered truthfully, as she stepped back to allow him entrance into her home.

Whittier glanced around the hall, eyes sliding quickly from doorway to stairs and back again. He stepped swiftly into her apartment, taking control of the door and closing it quickly. He arrested its motion with barely an inch of space remaining, gazing back the way he had come. Satisfied that no one was watching, he quietly closed the gap.

Gwen moved into the living room, maintaining a careful distance between herself and this self-avowed enemy.

The man looked slightly deranged. His greying hair was mussed, his manner of dress slipshod. He was out in his bedroom slippers, for heaven's sake. Whittier advanced into the living room, then stopped, fingers fidgeting with the buttons of his worn overcoat.

"I hardly know where to begin, Miss Vaughan." His glance skittered around the room, touching every item, but lingering on none. His gaze avoided her face. "I... uh, I've treated you unfairly."

At last he looked at her, and Gwen saw naked fear coiling in the depth of his eyes. "I didn't realize it until recently. I didn't realize a lot of things until recently."

He drew a shuddering breath, tears forming in his eyes. "I'm afraid it's too late. But I... I needed to warn you... to make you understand."

"Warn me about what, Dr. Whittier?" Gwen maintained her distance from him, but kept her voice clear and calm.

"You won't understand, but I've been under an evil influence. An ancient evil." He licked his lips, gaze darting around the room.

"Still am. Only now she controls my body, so she no longer needs to control my mind. I can think clearly now. I just can't stop my limbs from obeying her. I don't know why she allowed me to come here. Maybe she doesn't know."

The pitch of his voice rose, hysteria threatening to overtake him.

"Stay away from me, Miss Vaughan. Transfer out of my class. If you see me on campus, run away. She means to kill you. She'll use me to do it. I know you don't understand."

He laughed, the sound harsh and humorless.

"How could you? You must think I'm a lunatic." He dropped into a chair, burying his head in his hands. "Maybe I am. All I know is I'm in hell, and there's no escape."

"And if there were a way out?" Renzo asked, dropping the invisibility sigil and making his way to the morose man. "Would you truly welcome it?"

Whittier jumped from his chair. He tripped over an end table in an attempt to get his back against a wall as far from Renzo as possible.

"Where did you come from?" he asked, eyes wide. "Who are you?"

He glanced at Gwen, his eyes darting back to Renzo. "Miss Vaughan? You said we were alone!"

"I said there was no one in sight. Please sit down, Dr. Whittier," she said gently, "we may not have much time. This is Lorenzo Santini. My companion. You are in no danger from us."

Whittier moved cautiously back to the chair and perched on its edge, keeping his eyes focused on Renzo. "Where did he come from?"

Renzo moved into the room and sat beside Gwen on the couch, facing Whittier. "I've been here the whole time. Like Lilith, I am a magical being." He glanced at Gwen. "Unlike Lilith, I am here to protect Miss Vaughan."

Turning his full attention to Whittier, Renzo studied the man's face. "If you truly wish to be released from Lilith's influence, I'll do everything I can to free you. You must tell me how she ensnared you. Leave nothing out, the smallest detail could be the key to your freedom."

Hope dawned in Jason Whittier's eyes. He licked his lips and, haltingly, told his tale.

Gwen sat quietly, unwilling to break the spell of confidence Renzo was weaving so expertly. She was certain the aging professor would be unwilling to describe his debasement if he remembered she was in the room.

The scenes he described were so vivid Gwen could almost see them happening. She closed her eyes and watched Lilith lure her victim, ensnare his mind, then callously show him his degradation when he was beyond escape.

Gwen had known for months that Lilith was depraved, but it was horrible to see her malice and lack of empathy so clearly displayed in Whittier's words. Gwen had no reason to care about Jason Whittier, he had done nothing but make her life miserable since their first meeting, but she ached for his misery.

Listening to his tale, she realized that somewhere along the way, High Magic's cause had become her own.

She wasn't searching for the signs simply because they were her assigned task. She wasn't setting herself up against Lilith merely to spare the lives of college friends in Boulder. She wasn't even embracing the *Old One* life to impress Renzo, or Dylan, or even Merlin.

Gwen was doing all these things to protect innocent mortals. Unsuspecting people, like Jason Whittier, who weren't necessarily nice or high-minded. Simple mortal human beings who deserved to live their lives and make their choices without being forced into untenable situations by magical beings.

Beings they were defenseless against.

In the dark places of her mind, Gwen had wondered why she was working so hard to live up to the *Old Ones'* expectations.

Now the fully formed answer came to her, framed in glorious light.

This— obedience to High Magic and its defense of humanity— was her destiny.

How ironic that the answer came embodied in a man she didn't even like.

She was a defender of mankind, and would do everything in her power to see that her people— the people who had given her life — were safe from persecution by would-be gods.

Lilith… or anyone else.

Whittier finished his narrative and gazed at Renzo in mute appeal.

Renzo stood, walked to the window and stared into the darkness. When he turned back to the room, his face was bleak.

"I won't lie to you, professor. You have given Lilith power over your body through an ancient and powerful magic. It's not a spell I can break, or even counter." He returned to the couch and sat across from the unhappy human. "That said, I want you to know there is still hope. I will tell my people of your situation. Perhaps one of them will remember something that has escaped my attention."

Crestfallen, Dr. Whittier seemed to fold inward into a knot of pain.

"If it's any consolation," Renzo continued, "you have given the Light valuable information to help combat Lilith's evil."

"What do I do now?" Whittier raised haunted eyes to Renzo's face.

"You continue with your life." Gwen rejoined the conversation, her voice light and lyrical after the low, painful tones of Whittier's story. "Don't be concerned for my safety. I am well protected. Instead, be careful not to give Lilith cause to harm you further."

"Gwen's right, Jason. Don't antagonize Lilith. Give us time to formulate a plan. For the moment, she needs you as a fully functional man. Obey her. If she transforms you into one of her goblins, you will truly be beyond our help."

"Goblins?" Whittier's eyes widened. "There are worse things she can do to me? Without killing me, I mean?"

Renzo nodded solemnly. "Much worse. Tread warily."

Whittier closed his eyes, his face wreathed in despair. After a moment, he stood and walked to the door.

Gwen walked with him, touching the doorknob before he could open it. "Remember, Dr. Whittier," she said with an encouraging smile, "whenever you see me, you can be sure Renzo is nearby. Don't despair. Someone among our kin will know what to do."

"Blessings upon you, Jason." Renzo raised his hand as Gwen opened the door and the man stepped into the hall.

Dr. Whittier stood framed in the doorway, a wry smile on his lips. "I hope your blessing can reach me."

Straightening his shoulders, the aging man turned and walked away.

CHAPTER 23

*A*rranging her schedule so she could take the day off at Samhain was more difficult than Gwen had imagined. Halloween— Samhain's alter ego— fell on a Thursday this year, and preparing to miss classes for even a single day was an organizational nightmare.

Deciding it was easier to avoid asking for permission, she simply announced that she had a family engagement she needed to attend. After two weeks of determined effort, she had all of her papers completed and submitted in advance, her study groups appeased, and her shift at the museum covered.

On Wednesday night, everything was in order, but Gwen was tired and more than a little grumpy. "I certainly hope this Samhain gathering is worth the effort. Why do we have to be at the redwood grove before dawn? I could really use some extra sleep in the morning."

Renzo smiled sympathetically. "You'll feel better once you get there. The grove's innate magic and Samhain's heightened power will refresh you. Trust me."

She played with the remains of her roast beef and fried potatoes, pushing them around her plate with her fork.

"Besides, you haven't found your next clue yet. I'd think you'd be anxious to get to the gathering to see if someone there is holding it for you."

"I am," she growled, eyes blazing. "The lack of a clue is just one more irritation… and I've had way too many of them this week."

Dropping her fork with a clatter, she leaned back and huffed. "I need a rest. Not another day full of unknown responsibilities."

Recognizing Renzo's expression as wary readiness, she sighed heavily. "I'm sorry, Renzo. I'm overextended; stretched too thin. I'll be better after a full night's sleep." She tried to smile, but doubted the expression was anything but brittle. She was almost too tired to care.

Renzo reached across the table and touched her hand. "Go to bed, Gwen. Everything is under control. Rest. I'll wake you when it's time to leave."

With a curt nod, she rose from the table and stumbled to her room.

RENZO EYED the remains of dinner with resignation. He sketched a concise sigil and moved to stand by the large living room window while the mess cleared itself.

He was worried about Gwen.

She was wearing herself out physically and holding herself tightly in check emotionally.

The frantic pace she kept was common in academic settings—he'd been on enough campuses around the world in his centuries of existence to know that she would adapt to the pace, that it was a passing thing. The year or two of inordinate stress would make the work-a-day world feel tame once she left the crucible of this doctoral program.

She'd find her stride, would learn to relax when an opportunity for fun presented itself.

No, what worried him most was that the tight rein she held on her emotions was robbing her of the ability to relax in the moment.

"Is she afraid to have fun?"

The question hit the glass of the window and bounced back in his face.

Afraid to have fun?

Maybe that was exactly the problem. She had been enjoying herself the night she was attacked. Was her subconscious protecting her by not allowing her to take time out for recreation?

He knew for a fact she was terrified by the thought of sex.

The panic-ridden expression that suffused her face whenever their banter... or caresses... generated heat tore at his soul.

He loved her.

He wanted her.

But he had no idea how to counter the fear he saw sinking its claws ever deeper into her psyche. Maybe Merlin or Minerva would be able to counsel him tomorrow.

Too few hours later, Renzo knelt at Gwen's bedside in the gentle predawn light. He watched the easy rise and fall of her breathing, and enjoyed the sweet repose on her sleeping features. He longed for the day when she would feel as safe in the waking world.

"Gwen." He stroked her cheek gently as he said her name. "Wake up, sweetheart. That's the way. Come on, baby. Wake up."

HIS VOICE MERGED into her dream and she stretched lazily, enjoying his presence in her dream world. She wasn't afraid of his touch here. She'd like to stay, find out what loving him would be like. But... someone was calling her.

Someone needed her attention.

The real Renzo was calling.

She abandoned the comfort of her dream and swam to consciousness... to Renzo.

Gwen woke with an easy smile. "I heard you calling me. Is it time to go?"

"It is," he whispered. He smiled, a content, at-ease expression that warmed her heart.

"It's going to be a glorious day. I can almost smell the sweet mustiness of the redwoods from here." Renzo inhaled deeply, savoring an imagined aroma.

Giggling, Gwen pushed him lightly and rolled from the bed. "What shall I wear? Jeans or robes?"

"You look fine just the way you are." Renzo's eyes sparkled as his gaze travelled over her, from head to toe.

She shivered, still close enough to her dream to enjoy his frank appreciation of her form... which a quick glance in the mirror revealed to be distinctly sleep tousled. Her blue and white pajamas were wrinkled and askew; her hair was matted on one side, and her face still retained creases from the folds of her pillow case.

But Renzo didn't seem to mind. He made her feel beautiful.

"Be serious," she said, attempting to sound stern, though her heart sang. "What's appropriate? Jeans or robes?"

"Robes," he sighed. "Don't forget your sandals, belt and staff. This is a full ceremonial occasion."

CHAPTER 24

*O*nce properly attired, Gwen and Renzo teleported to the center of a grove of ancient coastal redwoods. The friendly giants lifted their proud heads to the early morning light and took little notice of the tiny figures clustered among their roots.

"Welcome, Kinsmen."

Merlin stood well above the forest floor on a root-gnarl of one of the ancient trees.

"The first light of Samhain is now upon us. Enjoy this day of rest and rejuvenation. Allow the power of this day and the magic of this enchanted grove to heal your spirits and refresh your souls. Mingle with old friends. Strive to establish new bonds."

He raised his staff in blessing as the captivating melody she had first heard at Beltane drifted through the grove.

"We will gather again at dusk for our sacred ritual."

Renzo and Gwen wandered among their clan for more than an hour. They enjoyed hot cocoa and scones at one of the food pavilions nestled unobtrusively among the fortress-like roots of a forest elder. Gwen exchanged hugs with Mei and Phoebe, and allowed Minerva to scan her body for signs of poor health.

"You're in excellent physical condition," Minerva said upon exiting her healing trance.

She studied Gwen's face intently. "But you are suffering from stress. I prescribe a day among the ancient redwoods. On a major arcane high day, if possible." She laughed at her own joke and hugged Gwen. "Blessings upon you, little sister."

Renzo stood across the grove talking to Dylan, Merlin, Kunto, Omar, and a tall, willowy man Gwen hadn't met. She approached them quietly, not wishing to interrupt their discussion.

"Any suggestions as to how I can help this man?" Renzo asked as Gwen joined them. He reached out and pulled her into the circle of conversation.

"I'm afraid I have to agree with your assessment, Lorenzo." Merlin's eyes were dark with anger. "I can think of nothing to counter the old magic Lilith has employed."

"Actually, there is a way," the tall *Old One* said. His voice was low and melodic, his words oddly soothing.

"But first," he turned to Gwen, fixing her with a sea-green gaze, "we have not met, Lady. I am Taliesin. I was unable to attend the Beltane fires, and so did not witness your initiation. Welcome to our family, Lady Guinevere." As he spoke, Taliesin bowed low and kissed the hand Gwen had proffered for a handshake.

"I am honored, Lord." Gwen swept a low curtsy. "I have known your name since long before I awoke to your world." Formalities observed, she peered eagerly into his face. "Can you really help Dr. Whittier?"

"There is indeed a way. But it will be very difficult to manage." He frowned and looked at Merlin. "Do you not think a drop of Lilith's blood encased in an ensorcelled crystal would be equal to the task?"

Merlin's jaw opened and closed a few times, but no sound emerged. A bubble of silence encased the group as the two elder *Old Ones* concentrated on Jason Whittier's dilemma.

At last, Merlin nodded. "Yes. That would certainly free him from her web. Ignoring for a moment the impossibility of gaining her blood, he would have to be warned never to remove the amulet. For any reason. The moment he took it off, she would regain her control... and her fury would be terrible indeed."

Taliesin turned to Renzo. "I can supply you with a properly spelled crystal vial."

Renzo's eyes widened and he opened his mouth to speak. Taliesin held up his hand to forestall him.

"You must understand, only Whittier can place the drop of blood in the vial. Just as she received a piece of his living self, so he must be the recipient of her living essence. You may help him obtain it, but he must be the one to actually place it in the vial."

Dylan glanced at Renzo and shook his head. "I can't imagine how you will get her to part with a drop of blood. Especially in the presence of a mortal." He licked his lips before continuing. "Try not to lose your own life in your attempt to help this man."

Gwen shivered, stepping closer to Renzo. Taliesin had outlined an unimaginable task, but it offered a ray of hope.

Perhaps they could outsmart Lilith, but the puzzle of how to get a drop of her blood without dying in the process would keep them plotting for quite a while.

Renzo shook himself, and then bowed to his kinsmen. "Thank you for your help. I think Gwen and I will wander for a bit while we contemplate this possibility." He took Gwen's hand firmly in his and led her away from the *Old Ones* congregated in the grove's center.

After a few paces, he stopped and smiled down at her. "Are you up for a ramble through the redwoods?"

She gazed into the forest ahead of them before gazing up into his eyes. "I'd love it. I've never seen anything like this forest before."

"Awesome, isn't it?" he asked, looking not at the trees, but at her. "Come on, let's explore. Just the two of us."

CHAPTER 25

*G*wen and Renzo walked into the forest on silent feet.

The trees surrounding them were almost entirely redwood. Here and there a few hemlock sprouted from the decaying forms of fallen giants. Because the ground under the massive trees was nearly always moist and shady, few plants grew there. Though the forest floor was far from clear, there was little variety in the plant life.

They strolled across a dense carpet of sorrel and redwood violets. At this time of year, the view was all shades of green and brown. But Gwen was sure that in the spring the violets and sorrel would provide a tapestry of color beneath the canopy of the enormous trees.

Enormous. That was an apt description.

Gwen had never seen trees like this. Not in Portland with its lush growing conditions, and not on the ranch in Colorado. The old growth forests on the mountains of Colorado had seemed huge when she was growing up, but they were comprised of normal evergreens. These redwoods... their majesty defied description.

She was surrounded by trees that ranged from 150 to 350 feet tall. She estimated that some of the trunks were 20 feet in diameter. If she didn't know she was on California's northern coast, she might believe she'd been transported into another dimension.

Renzo stopped beside a fallen tree, its surface covered with moss, sorrel and violets. The top of the horizontal trunk stood higher than his head. "Makes you feel like you're in another universe, doesn't it?"

"It does," Gwen agreed, her voice hushed. Even though there was no one near, she hated to disturb the serenity of this place.

"It's like being inside a cathedral. Only more so." She gave a soft snort of laughter. "That made no sense. But, somehow, this is more reverent than any human structure I've ever been in."

Renzo nodded and pulled her over to sit next to him on a large root shelf. The ledge, covered in soft vegetation like the fallen tree, bridged the gap between the downed giant and the redwood growing beside it and provided a comfortable spot to rest and enjoy the sunlight as it filtered through the grove's canopy.

Gwen closed her eyes, absorbing the calm serenity of the place. Peace saturated her soul; she was safe among these gentle giants. The magic of the grove surrounded and supported her, while the power of Samhain augmented the grove's majesty. Though her eyes remained closed, she was aware of the lines of power dancing firm and true along the limbs above her. Twisting and tangling as the breeze moved the branches, always popping resiliently back to their original paths.

Sigils woven from these lines would form powerful spells. Gwen imagined limitless possibilities in this place.

Opening her eyes, she found Renzo studying her face. The rich chocolate of his eyes was so warm, so inviting. She turned and drew his face to hers. The kiss was gentle. Exactly as she'd hoped it would be. He tasted of blueberry scones… with the intoxicating spice of masculine heat. He lifted his head, and she saw desire spark before he quickly buried it.

"Don't do that." Her voice was low and husky. "Not this time."

The sound sent shivers through Renzo's soul. "Don't do what? You kissed me." He fought to keep his voice calm, his tone measured, but it was hard. So very hard to hold himself in check this close to her. In this perfect space and time.

"That's not what I meant." Gwen smiled as she traced his mouth with her thumb. "Don't pull away from me. Don't hide behind that mask."

Renzo held her hand, interlaced their fingers, to stop her thumb's seductive movement. "I'm wearing that mask to protect you. I don't want to frighten you… no more than you already are."

He gazed deep into her eyes. "Don't ask me to take it off unless you're ready to see what's behind it." His voice sounded gruff; he was losing his battle for calm. He needed to either hold her tightly, or move away from her. This pretended casualness was costly.

"I love you, Renzo. Put the mask away." Gwen felt a wonderful lightness of spirit. A glorious clarity washed over her as she recognized the truth of her own words. "I'm safe here. I've always been safe with you."

Renzo didn't require additional encouragement. He kissed her, ending the conversation.

The kiss wasn't gentle this time, but it was still exactly what Gwen wanted… and needed. He took her mouth with hot, demanding, pent-up desire.

Quickly and deliberately they abandoned their clothes. Gwen would have rushed back into Renzo's arms, but he held her at a distance. She quivered, an intoxicating mixture of anxiety, anticipation and desire flaming through her blood.

He studied her, his gaze devouring every inch of her form, and she reveled in the knowledge that this strong, virile man— a man who had lived for centuries— desired her.

Renzo took his time, savoring his first unimpeded view of her body... and what he saw took his breath away. She was even more lovely than he'd imagined, more perfect than he'd dreamed.

And this vision, this manifestation of the goddess was giving herself to him.

Blessed be!

Had a luckier man— mortal or *Old One*— ever lived?

When he'd locked the memory of this moment in his centuries-long memory, Renzo met Gwen's gaze, and they flowed together. Two separate bodies whose life forces joined in a single raging flood.

Their time had come.

The calm serenity of the redwoods supported Gwen when her fears tried to surface, tried to stifle her delight in Renzo's attentions. She tensed momentarily as she speared each nasty thought with an arrow of light. Her battle won, she relaxed and wrapped herself around her lover.

Renzo, sensing her tension, grew still and looked questioningly into her eyes. When she answered his unspoken concern with a triumphant smile, he buried himself in her soft curves. This was what he'd been waiting for, and not just while she healed.

This was the connection, the completeness he'd been searching for through the long centuries of his life. Here was the core of his being.

Here was the completion of his power.

As they strained together toward the apex of their first climactic union, the world melded in a raging inferno. Renzo no longer knew where he ended and Gwen began, but he was conscious of their fusion.

Hot, delicious, painful, wonderful… complete oneness.

Their lines of power commingled forming a magical union reflecting their physical consummation.

Holding her in his arms in the aftermath, Renzo knew they would never truly be separate again. Gwen was part of him now.

They hadn't simply had sex, they had exchanged pieces of their essence.

This was exquisite magic; compelling and keen and ancient beyond his ability to comprehend.

They had chosen to come together in a sanctified place, on one of the most powerful days of the year.

Without conscious thought, they had poured themselves onto the redwood altar and made a sacrifice of their love, their lives. Their unintended reenactment of an ancient rite of wild magic had consecrated their new life, their conjoined life— at the birth of the *Old One* year.

An auspicious beginning indeed.

"I love you, Guinevere Enid Vaughan." Renzo murmured, as he lay beside her gazing up into layers of green. "Samhain begins our New Year. We're starting our life together at the beginning of the magical year." He kissed the top of her head. "Happy New Year, my love."

Gwen snuggled closer to Renzo, lazily stroking his chest. "Happy New Year, beloved. And... thank you for your patience. This was perfect."

"Indeed. It was." A voice croaked unfamiliar words from a throat unused to such exercise.

Renzo bolted upright, instinctively placing himself between the voice and the woman he loved...

...but there was no one there.

Warily, he surveyed the forest.

"Rest. Safe. Lady Guinevere." The voice croaked awkwardly.

This time Gwen found its source. Peering around Renzo's body, she spotted the bird sitting on the fallen redwood a few yards from them. She tapped Renzo's arm, pointed to the bird, and stretched to retrieve her discarded robe.

"Greetings, Master Jay. How may we be of service?" Gwen addressed the Stellar's Jay while Renzo shrugged into his own robe.

Similar in size to a common bluejay, the Stellar's Jay's coloration shimmered from iridescent black at the head to royal blue at the tail. Cocking its head to one side, the bird stared at Gwen with one beady black eye.

"My service. High Magic awaits. You conquered fear. Your clue is here." The bird's word's were choppy. It clearly required great effort to push them out.

"My fear?" Gwen looked puzzled. "Oh. You mean fear of sex?" She blushed, then grinned happily. "Yes. That's definitely gone.

Wait a minute. You can't mean High Magic was waiting for me to sleep with Renzo before it gave me the next clue. What if it hadn't happened today?"

"Opportunity missed."

Gwen stared, eyes wide with disbelief. "That's ridiculous. My whole quest would've been for nothing?" She turned a glare on Renzo. "Did you know my quest hinged on us making love?"

"Absolutely not," Renzo said, shaking his head. "It kind of makes sense though. High Magic expects us to conquer our fears." He gave her a silly grin. "High Magic knew this" he nodded toward the depression in the sorrel, "was up to you. Heck, I've been ready since... well, I've been ready for a long time." He hugged her tightly and kissed her quickly.

Mollified, Gwen addressed herself to the bird. "Okay. Where's my clue?"

Cocking its head to the other side, the bird answered. "Australia. Ayers Rock. Samhain. Dawn."

"Dawn. It's almost noon..." She jumped up in alarm as she realized the bird was flying away. "Wait. How do I know when it's dawn in Australia? Jay! Answer me."

The reply drifted into her mind like a feather floating to the earth. *Think, child. Seek in time... as well as space...*

Renzo stared after the departing bird for a long moment before turning to face Gwen, his expression concerned. "Did it answer you?"

Gwen started. She had momentarily forgotten Renzo's existence. Stunned by High Magic's parting thought, Gwen's mind raced.

The possibilities of being able to seek in time astounded her.

Turning her attention to Renzo, she smiled, her heart overflowing with jubilation.

This man, this *Old One* was her mate. Her match, her equal. And she had found him very early in what would be an eternal existence.

Even by human standards, twenty-two was young to find one's soul mate; but seen in the light of *Old One* immortality... well, the thought was staggering, but true nonetheless.

Renzo belonged to her, and she to him.

"Not the jay, High Magic. It seems I can seek in time as well as space." She threw herself into Renzo's arms. "No wonder High Magic wasn't concerned about the timing of my healing. The signs would wait for me. I had no idea..."

Her voice trailed off as Renzo tightened his embrace. Powerful new sensations flooded her, but she had no trouble recognizing their message.

She wanted him.

Again.

Now.

"If the signs will wait," he murmured against her neck, "let them." His questing lips found hers — and her answer.

They sank back into the fragrant sorrel, the quest momentarily forgotten.

CHAPTER 26

*I*n the early afternoon, Renzo and Gwen strolled back to the gathering in the center of the grove. They stopped at one of the food pavilions and enjoyed a late lunch with friends, then went in search of Merlin.

They found him near his root-gnarl platform, engaged in a harp duel with Taliesin. The music those two ancient bards drew from their Celtic harps was indescribable. Arrowing straight past Gwen's logical mind to paint scenes in her soul.

Glorious battles bathed in the shining light of victory emblazoned themselves in her mind, while acknowledging the terrible price that had been paid. The suffering. The lost possibilities of lives that would never be lived; of children that would never be conceived. The agony conducted a grim counterpoint to the glory.

Indeed, the price made the victory glorious... that *Old Ones* and mortals were willing to suffer such cost in order to attain victory. Truly, a divine mystery to be puzzled over for ages yet to come.

When the last chords died away, Merlin and Taliesin sat with bowed heads. A moment of silence too sacred to break descended on their audience.

At last the two bards rose, bowed to each other and called for flagons of mead. Immediately the desired drinks appeared and the spell was broken.

Gwen and Renzo shouldered their way through the crowd to Merlin's side.

"Blessings, Lord." Gwen inclined her head. When she looked up she caught a twinkle deep in Merlin's eyes.

"Blessings, Lady." He broke into a wide grin. "But I thought we had agreed to dispense with such formality between us?"

Color raced into Gwen's face, but she managed a quick-witted reply. "Formality has its place. After the mastery you just exhibited, I could hardly be flip. But since you remind me of our agreement..." she threw herself into his arms and hugged him fiercely.

Merlin was momentarily stunned by her rapid tactical change. His surprise lasted only an instant, then he laughed heartily and swung his youngest kinswoman in a wide circle. When he set her on her feet again, he beamed broadly.

"Gwen, I swear. You never cease to amaze me." He held her at arms length and studied her glowing face. He turned a shrewd gaze on Renzo who stood nearby watching intently.

"Something has changed," he muttered under his breath.

Focusing on Gwen again he said aloud, "Was there something you needed from me? Other than a good solid hug?"

Gwen hooted with laughter. "I've come to tell you that I've found my Samhain clue. I'm to search Ayers Rock— in Australia— at dawn on Samhain."

Seeing the look of consternation cross his face did her heart good. She wasn't the only one who thought the clue a little late in coming. "I know, it sounds like the moment has passed. But High Magic assures me that I can search in time as well as space."

Merlin's eyes widened with surprise. "Truly? That's a rare gift."

"That's what I told her." Renzo entered the conversation. "She wants to search right now, before the twilight ceremonies. Do you have time to accompany us?"

Before he could answer, Gwen intervened. "Renzo's being over cautious. You and Mei and Dylan don't need to leave the festival. Renzo can use the augmentation sigil to protect me from human interference. That worked perfectly well last time."

Merlin studied Gwen's shining face before turning his attention to Renzo's frowning one, and chuckled. "As usual, I see that Lorenzo is erring on the side of caution, while Gwen is trying to throw it to the wind.

"Frankly, Gwen, I'm delighted to see you so full of confidence again. I have been concerned about you. However, I must side with Renzo." He patted her shoulder and moved away. "Gather the others and meet me at the divided redwood to the north of the grove in about twenty minutes. We have plenty of time before sunset."

Renzo grinned. "Why don't we split up? You look for Mei, and I'll find Dylan. See you at the tree."

He sprinted away before she could unleash the storm brewing in her eyes.

The five Old Ones met by the lightning-divided giant twenty minutes later. Gwen took her place in the center of a loose circle formed by the other four. She closed her eyes, aware of the light mind-touches established by each of her friends. They were already arranged in their warding positions and would follow her flight in formation. Merlin wanted no interference with her quest this time.

Gwen closed her mind to niggling worries about the feasibility of time searches. If High Magic said it was possible, it was possible.

Instead she concentrated on dawn. Samhain dawn. At Ayers Rock.

Instantly time and space fled before her vision.

There! Shining in the first rays of the sun.

On the very top of a sandstone monolith that changed color as she watched.

She threw herself into the void that loomed between her physical being and that shine... and she stood before it, stretching out her hand, unaware of anything beyond the glowing object in the circle of her fingers. She closed her fist, felt a burning tingle as the sign of fire coalesced in her flesh and blood grasp.

Snapping back to her usual senses, she found herself not on Ayers Rock at all. She still stood in the redwood grove, encircled by her friends and lover. Glancing down she opened her fist and examined the small solid object that had so recently blazed in the southern hemisphere.

"What's wrong?" Renzo demanded, breaking ranks and striding to Gwen. "Why didn't you go?"

Gwen looked up, puzzled. "But I did." she whispered, holding up the sign of fire, burning red-gold in the late afternoon sun. "I did."

CHAPTER 27

"Hello? Aunt Katie?" Gwen's face beamed as she heard her aunt's voice over the telephone. "How are you? Is everything all right on the ranch? I've missed you so much." She listened for a moment, nodding her head as Katie responded from Colorado. "I can hardly wait for Thanksgiving. It's going to be so wonderful to be home."

Renzo smiled as he listened to her end of the conversation. He knew she was working up to the big question.

"Yes, I've already made my airline reservations. I'll email my itinerary to you. Uhm... Aunt Katie? Would it be all right if I bring someone with me?" Gwen's eyes were bright and there were spots of color high on her cheekbones. She was trying to be casual about this trip home, but Renzo understood its importance. This was as close as she could come to taking him home to meet her parents. Katie and Jem's blessing was desperately important to her. They would never understand who she was, the *Old One* they had helped to raise, but their opinion and love remained the foundation of her life.

"Okay. That sounds great. We'll see you at DIA on the twenty-fifth. What?" She paused to listen once again. "His name? Of course, he has a name. It's Lorenzo Alan Santini." She turned to look at him, and the love shining in her eyes took his breath away.

"You're going to love him, Aunt Katie. I do."

The end of the conversation was drowned out by Renzo's pulse drumming in his ears. She loved him. They were a couple now. She was his. It wasn't a dream. It was an indisputable fact.

She came to sit with him on the couch when the call ended.

Putting an arm around her shoulders, he asked, "So, how did it go? Do I get to spend Thanksgiving at the ranch? Or do I have to spend the whole visit in invisible mode?"

Gwen laughed and elbowed him in the ribs. "Of course you're coming to the ranch. Aunt Katie is very excited to meet you. She'll spoil you rotten, and pry mercilessly into your private life."

Pulling his face to hers, she indulged in a long, slow kiss.

He responded by deepening the kiss and tightening his embrace. The freedom to hold her, to love her… absolutely incredible.

When the kiss ended, she curled into his arms and sighed contentedly. "Thanks for coming to Colorado with me. I think this initial meeting will be easier for Uncle Jem on his own territory."

They'd discussed inviting her foster parents to come to Portland for the holiday— Gwen wanted them to meet Renzo and see her new apartment— but after thinking it through had decided that Katie and Jem would be happier meeting Renzo at the ranch. After all, Renzo and Gwen lived together. Her foster parents deserved to get to know him before they were faced with that fact.

Besides, Renzo understood Gwen's need to visit the ranch with him, to see how he fit into the puzzle of her life. The ranch might be her past, while their love, their conjoined fates, represented the future, but Gwen still needed to observe how he meshed with the people and places that had shaped her life.

He couldn't show her his past, but he could certainly make an effort to fit into hers.

CHAPTER 28

*D*avid stared around the single's bar. What on earth was he doing here?

Who was he kidding?

He knew the answer. Two answers, really.

The obvious one was that Joey had grabbed his arm and dragged him out of his apartment. His friend had insisted, pointing out that David was turning into a hermit, that he needed to get a life.

But that wasn't the real reason.

The real reason he was in this smoky, loud, gaudy bar was that he had let the only woman who'd ever meant anything to him walk out of his life.

He picked up the shot of whiskey and stared into its amber depths. He didn't really think it held any answers. God knew he'd downed enough of the stuff in the past six weeks.

Why did she have to be so stubborn? Why did she have to bring up love and marriage in the first place? What sane couple got married these days without living together first?

They'd had a good thing going.

They were good for each other.

Now nothing was good.

Work was dull and colorless, like trying to enjoy impressionist art through black and white photographs.

Everything he ate tasted like cardboard. Didn't matter what it was or who prepared it— food tasted like cardboard. Six weeks of eating cardboard was enough to throw anyone into depression.

He had no personal life. When he wasn't at work, he sat in front of the TV, drinking swill and eating cardboard.

The only thing that scraped through his colorless existence was the liquid fire contained in a shot glass.

David downed the whiskey as Joey elbowed him in the ribs.

"I don't know why you get all the luck. Check out the babe." Joey nodded toward a dark-haired beauty at the end of the long mahogany bar. "She's been making eyes at you. I tried to inter-cept the look, but no go. You're the one she wants."

David glanced at the woman. Even through the alcohol-haze in his brain and smoke in the room, he could see she was hot. Why would a woman like that be interested in a miserable drunk like him?

He established eye contact with her... and a charge of electricity jolted through his body.

Why was a fine specimen of masculinity like himself sitting alone at a bar? He was a god among insects. He could have any woman he wanted— and he wanted only the finest.

And women certainly didn't come any finer than that one. Look at those big blue eyes. Not to mention all the other assets she showed off to such advantage.

Unconsciously, David straightened on his bar stool. He squared his shoulders and watched with hot desire as Lilith rose from her seat and made her way toward him. As she shouldered through the crowd, a man stepped in front of her, breaking their eye contact.

Immediately, David slumped on the stool, his eyes reverting to the shot glass on the bar.

What was he doing? It wouldn't matter if that woman was a movie star with millions. She still wouldn't be Rachel.

He buried his head in his hands, cursing himself for an idiot. He was miserable without Rachel. Time to admit the truth: he loved her.

Whether he wanted to or not.

He gazed at his reflection in the mirror behind the bar. He looked like hell. He frowned. Pushing the shot glass away, he stood, determined to clean up and then find Rachel and beg her forgiveness.

If he was really lucky, maybe she'd still be crazy enough to want to marry him.

The mirror reflected a man with new found determination as he paid his tab and left the bar.

THE MIRROR also reflected an outraged *Old One*, thwarted by circumstance when she had been sure of her prey.

However, Lilith had no intention of letting a little thing like chance deprive her of this particular quarry.

WHEN DAVID OPENED his door an hour or so later to find the gorgeous brunette from the bar draped against his doorframe, his initial reaction was irritation.

"Aren't you going to invite me in?" Her voice was silken against his frayed nerves. When she flowed past him into his home, he was too stunned to protest.

"I like your place," the woman said, shaking her dark, luxurious hair.

David watched entranced as the strands settled in place over barely covered breasts. The midnight blackness of her hair contrasted richly with the creaminess of her skin. She was a visual feast to a man who had lived too long in a colorless world.

Forcing his attention away from her ample breasts, David swallowed hard. "Who are you? What do you want?"

Her blue eyes smoldered with desire, while those perfect red lips arched in a knowing smile.

"Isn't it obvious? What I want?" She sidled closer to David, placing a hand on his chest. "The question is... what do you want?" She drew her hand languorously down his body.

Testosterone raged through his system. His body responded with lightning speed; desire gripped his mind.

Lilith smiled, her expression veiled, but triumphant. This was too easy. This mortal was no match for her, but she would certainly enjoy binding him to her service.

With a masterful effort of will, David grabbed her hand and thrust her away.

Rachel. He needed to focus on Rachel, but it was hard to think. Waves of longing threatened to drown him. He forced himself to concentrate. No matter how seductive this woman was, she wasn't worth losing Rachel.

What was she doing here anyway?

As David's mind cleared, Lilith recognized her defeat.

"Puny mortal." She drew herself up to her full height, a dangerous fire flashing in her eyes. "You cannot escape my will." The smile that settled on her lips was calculating and cruel. "You've made a poor bargain. You would have enjoyed sacrificing to me. No one knows more about sexual satisfaction than the Queen of Darkness."

Lilith traced a sigil in the air, and David lost all knowledge of his body.

He was aware, but... disembodied. He could hear the words she spoke, but hearing was the only sense available to him. His body was an anchor, negating his soul's desired flight. There was no escape from this prison.

He was captive inside his own skull.

"Too late. You'll never use your body again. You should have used it to bring us both pleasure while you had the chance." She tapped one long, slender finger against her lips.

"I think you should contemplate your folly for a while." Lilith gave him a gentle push, and his seemingly lifeless body toppled to the floor. "How long do you think it'll take your human authorities to find you? A day? A week?

"No matter. Maybe I'll dig you up in a hundred years or so. Perhaps by then you'll be ready to play."

David's soul screamed, as Lilith laughed... and vanished.

CHAPTER 29

"*H*ave you seen David recently?" Rachel asked Gwen. She tried to sound unconcerned, but saying his name hurt. The two young women sat at two-top table in a small but chic downtown café. They met for lunch once a week, taking turns choosing the restaurant.

"Not since Friday. Why?" Gwen asked with a raised eyebrow

"Don't you see him everyday? At the museum, I mean."

"No." Gwen took a bite of her shrimp salad. "My work schedule at the museum is pretty haphazard." She pulled her organizer from her backpack. "This is the eleventh... I'm not due in 'til tomorrow afternoon." She replaced the organizer and sipped her raspberry lemonade. "Do you want me to give him a message?"

Color flooded Rachel's pale cheeks, and she took a hurried gulp of soda. A moment passed before she spoke. "No, nothing like that. It's just..."

She raised her eyes to Gwen's, silently pleading for understanding. "It's strange, but I have a really strong feeling that he's in danger." Leaning back in her chair, she closed her eyes. "Every time I relax, I hear him calling me... pleading for rescue. His anguish is almost unbearable."

She opened her eyes and glared at Gwen, defying her friend to belittle her fears. "It's been over six weeks since we broke up. I don't think this is just about missing him." She reached out and gripped Gwen's hand. "Help him, Gwen. I know he's in trouble."

Gwen studied Rachel's face, then raised her eyes to the other side of the room where Renzo sat on a bench in the café's waiting area reading a novel. He glanced up, met her gaze, and nodded. Getting to his feet, he ambled to their table.

"You won't mind if Renzo joins us, I hope?"

Rachel sat up and looked around, catching sight of Renzo as he wove through the tables to join them.

"Of course not. I was kind of wondering where he was."

As Renzo pulled a chair to their table, Gwen outlined Rachel's fears. "What do you think? Should we be concerned?"

Renzo gazed thoughtfully at Rachel. "I'll tell you what. If you'll promise to go back to the apartment with Gwen and wait for me, I'll run by the museum and check on him. I've been looking for a chance to chat with him anyway."

He turned a piercing stare on Gwen. "You have to promise to wait at the apartment. Close the wards when you get there, and stay put 'til I get back. I don't care what happens. Agreed?"

Gwen solemnly held up her hand in oath-taking position. "I promise. Come on, Rachel. Let's go home, so the man can do his work."

"Thanks, you guys." Rachel breathed a sigh of relief. "Thanks for taking this seriously."

IT TOOK LONGER than Gwen expected for Renzo to contact her. She was beginning to be a little on edge herself before she felt his delicate touch at the edge of her mind.

Gwen?

I'm here.

Is Rachel with you?

She is.

Move away from her.

Gwen didn't question his directive. "We could both do with a cup of tea. Wait right here while I put the kettle on."

Rachel didn't respond. She was resting on the couch with her eyes closed, willing David to be safe and healthy.

When Gwen was alone in the kitchen, she returned her attention to Renzo. *Did you find him?*

I did… and it's not a pretty sight.

Is he drunk or something?

Lilith.

The name, and all it implied, sent chills down Gwen's spine.

Is he alive? She waited breathlessly for his reply. She was concerned for David, but she was terrified for Rachel.

Barely. She's locked him in an enchantment so deep I almost couldn't detect his life force. I'm going to bring him home. Do your best to prepare Rachel.

Renzo? Can we save him?

I don't know. We'll discuss our options when I get there.

Renzo's touch left her mind, and Gwen strode resolutely to the living room.

"Rachel." She put a hand on her friend's shoulder and urged her into a sitting position. "Renzo found David. He's bringing him here."

Rachel's eyes widened in panic. "Oh, Gwen. I don't want to see him. I've got to go."

Gwen gripped her arm, preventing her from rising.

"He won't know you're here, Rachel. Lilith has him locked in an enchantment. Renzo could barely tell he's alive." Gwen kept her voice low and calm, but that didn't prevent Rachel from reacting.

All color drained from her face, she gasped as though she couldn't get enough oxygen, and her eyes glazed.

Fearing her friend was about to faint, Gwen pushed Rachel's head to her knees.

"Breathe, Rachel. That's it. In and out. You can do it." When she felt her friend begin to resist her downward pressure, Gwen released her.

"Sit up slowly." She studied Rachel's face, noting the return of color and the alertness of her eyes. Nodding, she said, "Just sit still while I get that tea."

By the time Gwen returned with the tea, Rachel was fully upright, her complexion pastier than usual, but no longer looking like she'd pass out.

Gwen placed a warm mug in Rachel's hand and encouraged her take a sip, hoping the warm liquid would help restore more of the color to Rachel's haggard face.

They'd barely had time to set their mugs on the coffee table when Renzo strode into the room, his face bleak but grimly determined. He moved straight to Rachel and sat beside her on the couch.

"If we break this enchantment, he will owe his life to you." He hugged her close, protecting her as sobs wracked her body. "If the human authorities had found him first... well, they'd not have been able to find the life in him."

Gwen moved to Rachel's other side and patted her back. An inadequate gesture, but the best she could manage.

"Don't despair, Rachel. He's alive." Renzo's voice was fierce as he held his anguished friend. "Gwen and I will find a way to free him. Lilith will not win this battle."

"I want... I want to see him." Rachel's words were torn by sobs, but her tear-stained face held staunch resolve.

Renzo nodded. "Of course. He's on the bed in the guest room." He gave Rachel a final hug, then released her.

She wavered slightly at the loss of his supporting strength, then stood and walked valiantly toward the bedroom.

Gwen squeezed Renzo's hand, kissed his cheek, and followed Rachel to David's bedside.

CHAPTER 30

*R*enzo and Gwen held silent council over Rachel's head as the petite blonde sat motionless beside the man she loved.

What can we do? Can we untangle the knot Lilith tied around his life force? Gwen peered intently at the mangled mess of power lines that bound David's body.

I don't think so. Even if we could manage to untangle that chaos, she's got it sealed in place. Renzo directed her mind to the impenetrable mark that sealed Lilith's work.

There's got to be something we can do. We can't just leave him like this. She stifled an urge to hit something, anything. She picked up a pillow, clutching it so tightly her knuckles whitened. Too bad it wasn't Lilith's neck. Throttling a decorative pillow couldn't assuage this unbearable tension, but she had to do something.

Of course we won't. Come on. He moved quietly toward the door. *I'll check the wards. You explain to Rachel that we're going to leave him in her care while we search the Gramarye library.* He glanced back at the corpse-like young man on the bed and the miserable young woman at his side. *We'll find the answer if we have to search every book in the library.*

~

AFTER THE OLD ONES LEFT, Rachel stood and walked to the window. She couldn't bear seeing David like this, his complexion pale and waxy, his breathing so shallow she couldn't detect it, and when she touched his hand, the skin was cold.

This wasn't the man she loved. What was on that bed was nothing but a shell.

Where was David? The real David?

Renzo assured her that David was still alive, but where?

Tears filled her eyes. She couldn't hold back the flood much longer. Burying a desperate howl behind her fists, she screwed her eyes as tightly shut as was physically possible. Her breathing came fast and shallow, the panting of an animal with a mortal wound.

When the storm could no longer be contained, she flung herself onto the bed beside the husk that had once housed her beloved David, and wailed out her grief, anger and frustration.

Once the bout of hysteria had passed, Rachel sat up and wiped away her tears.

"Oh, David. I was a fool. I should have accepted your love without condition." She leaned closer to his pale impassive face. "I love you. I'll always love you," she whispered, and kissed his silent lips.

She rested her aching head on his chest and wondered if Gwen could put her under a similar spell? Then she could wait for him in painless oblivion.

The emotional storm had left her exhausted and with a nasty headache. On top of that, she was so congested she couldn't breathe. The need for oxygen finally forced her from the bed in search of a tissue.

Rachel was in the bathroom when she heard it.

A soft, croaky noise. Rusty, like a long unused hinge forced back into service. Only it wasn't metallic. It sounded like a voice.

And it was calling her name!

Racing back to David's side, her heart pounding so hard it hurt, she cautioned herself not to put too much hope in what was undoubtedly a desperate delusion.

When she reached the door to his room and saw him lying exactly as he had been when she left, all her adrenaline deserted her and she nearly collapsed.

She was delusional after all.

Dragging herself across the room, she sat on the chair Renzo had placed next to the bed. With weary resignation, she rested her forehead on the edge of the bed and slipped her trembling fingers beneath David's motionless hand.

The moment she touched him, she heard another tortured word.

"Rachel."

His voice rasped— the sound seemed to ooze from a bleeding soul, but she heard it.

His hand was still cold, his body immobile, but he'd spoken her name... and she'd heard it!

"David?" Rachel jumped to her feet, caressed his face with her hands, and stroked his closed eyelids. "Oh David. Fight. Come back to me. I know you can do it. Please, David, don't leave me here alone."

She was babbling, but it didn't matter.

All that mattered was that David had spoken!

He was in there. He knew she was here. He would come back to her.

He had to.

"Come on, darling. Open your eyes. You can do it. Lilith can't beat us— not when we're together. David! Come back."

She leaned close to his face, her breath mingling with his, and willed him to open his eyes. She kissed him again, and this time felt his warm breath on her lips.

Rachel stood up, stared at the ceiling and shouted at the top of her lungs, "Gwen. Renzo. Wherever you are, come back. Gwen! He's trying to fight. Renzo! I need you. Oh please, come back."

She whirled around and jumped onto the bed beside David. "Come on, David. You can do this." She chafed his hands, stroked his hair, attempted chest compressions— anything to get his circulation going.

"I love you."

His words were breathy and barely there, but they were the sweetest music Rachel had ever heard.

"I love you too, David Milligan. I'll do anything you want. Just come back to me." She grabbed his hand and kissed his knuckles. "Fight it, David. Come all the way back."

❧

THE AIR behind Rachel shimmered as Gwen and Renzo appeared in the room.

"Rachel. What's happening?" Gwen ran to the bed and examined the magic lines that held David in restraint.

"I don't know. I just know he's spoken to me several times." Hope shone from her eyes as she glanced from Gwen to Renzo. "Help him. He's fighting. I know he is."

Renzo took Rachel by the shoulders and pulled her away from the bed. "Tell me what happened. Every detail. This shouldn't be possible. Some ancient magic is at work, and I need to know what it is."

While Rachel told him everything she could remember, Gwen scrutinized the sigils ensnaring David.

Yes. This time she was able to detect a pale glimmer of his consciousness. She stretched her awareness to the fringes of his mind and delicately probed that glimmer.

Before she realized what was happening, David's mind grabbed the silver tendril of her thought and refused to let go.

Don't leave me, Gwen. His mind-voice was soul-piercing in its desperation. *I can hear everything that's going on. I've been conscious since Lilith did this to me. I know what's happening. Don't leave me in the dark again.*

Rest easy. We won't leave you. I'll keep a light contact with you. Just push your thought along it if you need to get my attention. Gwen smiled and brushed her fingers through David's hair. *I must hear what Rachel's saying. I must know what has allowed you this much freedom.*

She kissed me. She got me all wet with her tears, and then she kissed me.

His thought was filled with wonder.

I can't feel anything else, but I felt her tears... and now I can feel when she touches me.

Rest and listen, David. I'll talk to Renzo. Reach out to me if you need me.

When Gwen turned to Renzo and Rachel, tears brimmed her eyes. "I've made contact with him. He can communicate with me by mindspeech."

Renzo released Rachel and strode to Gwen. "Does he know what happened?"

"Yes, he's been aware the whole time. Lilith left him helpless. He can hear, but that's all."

She turned to Rachel, hugging her fiercely. "It was your kiss— and your tears. That's what's made the difference. He felt your tears, and then you kissed him. Since then, he's been aware of your touch."

Her eyes shining, Gwen turned to Renzo. "This is Wild Magic. It's where all the legends of enchantments being broken by love's first kiss come from."

"But," Rachel looked up in surprise, "that can't be. That was hardly our first kiss."

Renzo laughed heartily, hope at last relieving his weary soul. "She did say they were legends. Wild Magic doesn't require that it be a *first* kiss— just that the love be true."

Rachel was, once again, sitting cross-legged on the bed beside David. She stroked his hair, his arm.

"He says that feels wonderful... please don't stop." Gwen smiled at Rachel's surprised expression, and turned to her own love. "What's next, Renzo?"

"You're safe, David. Lilith can't touch you here. Rest 'til morning, then we'll talk."

Renzo rose, reached for Gwen's hand, and the two of them stumbled from the room.

David lay still for a moment after they left. Then, moving with infinite care, he removed Rachel from his shoulder and sat up.

Rachel sighed, turning slightly in her sleep.

David smiled and tenderly brushed the hair from her cheek.

He was alive.

He had control of his body.

And it was all because of Rachel.

He'd been aware of Renzo's raging when the *Old One* found David in his apartment, apparently dead. Renzo had cried aloud that Rachel had been right.

Rachel had sent the *Old One* in search of him. Rachel— whose ears had seared through Lilith's spell. Rachel— whose kiss had broken the seal, allowing Renzo and Gwen to free him.

Everything came down to Rachel.

David was a very lucky man… and he loved Rachel, the woman who had been the key to his salvation.

Enjoying the play of muscles in a body he'd thought lost to him, David stood and walked to the window. Darkness greeted his eyes. He had no idea what time it was, didn't really care. He used his sense of sight; enjoying the subtle nuances of shading that played between the night and the dim remains of the city's

"Now we go to work untying these knots." He grinned at Gwen. "We couldn't do it before, but Rachel's kiss broke the seal. It's just a matter of time, now."

Renzo traced a sigil in the air and produced two comfortable chairs. He and Gwen settled themselves into them.

"Okay. Rachel, we're going to be very busy for a while. Please don't speak to us. David, unless you have an emergency, be content with Rachel's touch. Don't interrupt Gwen with questions."

"He understands," Gwen reported.

"So do I. Take as long as you need, just bring him back to me." Rachel stretched out on the bed next to David and put her head on his shoulder.

"Patience is a virtue," she whispered, "and I can be virtuous… for a little while longer."

CHAPTER 31

*D*avid's eyes snapped open. He could see again. H
darted around the room; he was right w
expected to be. He expelled a deep, shuddering sigh.

He was safe.

Rachel slept beside him, her head resting on his sh
wanting to disturb her, he contented himself with lif
hand and cautiously moving each finger.

"Welcome back, David," Gwen said softly. "You'r
fine."

He turned his attention to Gwen. She looked a
haunted, her skin stretched taught, with bluish
areas beneath her eyes. Her lips were cracke
she'd bitten them as she concentrated on her w

"Gwen and I need some rest," Renzo added, h
bleak with exhaustion. "I know you've beer
but I doubt you've gotten much rest.

At last, the invigoration of his release seeped away, to be replaced by soul-deep exhaustion. He returned to the bed and, drawing Rachel securely into his arms, fell headlong into a deep, peaceful sleep.

CHAPTER 32

*G*wen was happily frying bacon when Rachel appeared in the kitchen the next morning.

"What happened last night?" Rachel reached for a bacon strip and took a healthy bite. "I know David's all right— he's curled up in there snoring to beat the band— but tell me the details."

Gwen lifted several more slices from the pan with a deadly looking fork before answering. "Not much to tell. Renzo and I exhausted ourselves untying a really nasty magical snarl." She grinned at Rachel and snagged a piece of bacon for herself. "You know the kind, one you'd cut out of your hair rather than try to comb out. But it was worth it. As soon as we unknotted the tangle and released the magic, he opened his eyes and moved his hand."

"Why didn't you wake me?" Rachel asked, though the question sounded petulant, even to her own ears. "Sorry. You just said you were exhausted."

"You've got that right." Gwen shrugged. "You were asleep. David needed to rest, and we were dead on our feet. It didn't seem like the right time for a party."

Placing the platter of bacon on the table, Gwen stepped back to the stove and broke several eggs into the frying pan. As she expertly flipped the eggs, Renzo and David appeared, conjured by the mesmerizing smell of coffee, bacon and frying eggs.

David rubbed the sleep from his eyes and gazed around the room with a wide grin. "Man! Does it ever feel good to be standing up again."

His gaze landed on Rachel and he strode quickly to her side. "Thanks for bringing the cavalry to my rescue, Beautiful." Sweeping her into his arms, he kissed her heartily.

"Break it up. Give the woman some air." Gwen swatted him playfully on the arm with a dish towel. "Everybody ready for some chow?"

"I could eat a horse," David said eyeing the platters Gwen carried to the table, "but I'll make do with about a dozen of those eggs."

When everyone had taken the first edge off their hunger, David leaned back in his chair. "Thanks, guys. I owe you my life— each of you. I know it was a group effort, but I'm pretty sure you couldn't have pulled it off if any of you had been missing."

He made eye contact with each of them in turn, ending with Rachel... and held her gaze long enough that Renzo and Gwen began to be uncomfortable.

Just as they decided it was time to make a tactful exit, David spoke.

"Don't go. I want you to be part of this." David placed his napkin on the table and knelt beside Rachel's chair.

"Rachel Anne Carson, will you be my wife?"

The color drained from Rachel's face so fast David was afraid she might faint. Peripherally, he heard Gwen's sharp intake of breath and Renzo's involuntary snort.

"What?" he asked, looking from one *Old One* to the other, before focusing on Rachel exclusively.

"It's okay if you don't want to answer right now. I've been a jerk and I know it. I just want everyone to know where I stand. I love you, Rachel." His voice sounded distinctly defiant. This wasn't going as he'd imagined.

At last, Rachel found her voice.

"Do you?" she asked, staring directly into his eyes. "Do you really love me? I won't have you marrying me out of gratitude."

Her eyes swam with tears. "I deserve better. I deserve to be loved!"

David sprang upright, stalked to the window, then turned to face his friends.

"Is that what you think? That I don't know the difference between love and gratitude?"

Renzo rose and walked toward the younger man. "David, be reasonable. You've been through a terrifying ordeal. You need some time to get your bearings again."

"I've got my bearings," David growled. "Rachel is the center of my life."

Tears rolled down Rachel's cheeks, and David strode to her side. Taking her hands, he gazed into her eyes.

"I love you, Rachel. I've been an idiot, but I'd already realized that before Lilith screwed with me. In fact, I might have to thank her for waking me up."

"What?" Renzo and Gwen spoke simultaneously, but it was Gwen who continued the thought. "What do you mean? Had you seen Lilith before she came to your apartment?"

David looked up from Rachel, surprised by the intensity of Gwen's question.

"Yeah, sure, she came on to me in a bar. Joey had dragged me out of my apartment to a single's bar." He glanced at Rachel before continuing. "There was this really gorgeous brunette making eyes at me from the end of the bar. Joey noticed her before I did, but she wasn't interested in Joe.

"She and I made eye contact, and I felt like I was God's gift to women. Then, when she was coming toward me, a guy walked between us and we lost eye contact."

David paused, licked his lips, and staring at Rachel, said, "That's when I knew. It didn't matter how fabulous another woman might be... she could never be you."

He shivered and glanced at Gwen. "I got up, paid my tab and went home. I took a quick shower, shaved and was on my way to find Rachel to propose when Lilith arrived." David shrugged. "You know the rest."

Gwen gazed across the table at the friend who had nearly suffered Whittier's fate.

"Oh, wow, David. You have no idea how close you came. I guess Rachel saved you again."

But David wasn't interested in Lilith at the moment. He was only concerned with Rachel.

"So you see, it's got nothing to do with gratitude. I mean, I'm grateful, certainly. But I'm asking you to marry me because I can't imagine my life without you."

Dropping to one knee, he said, "Marry me, Rachel."

This time there was no hesitation. Rachel threw herself into his arms, tears streaming down her face, and cried, "Yes!" over and over again.

CHAPTER 33

*R*enzo was listening to Rachel and David argue good-naturedly over how soon the wedding would be, when he became aware of a gentle tug at the corner of his consciousness. Giving it his full attention, he found Taliesin waiting to speak to him.

Greetings, milord. Thank you for your attention. Taliesin's mind-speech was as melodious as his speaking voice. *Would this be an inconvenient time for a brief visit?*

Not at all, Lord. We would be honored. Renzo pictured his location for Taliesin's teleportation before he continued his thought. *We have a mortal couple with us, but they are aware of the existence of Old Ones. Actually, we would appreciate your help.* Renzo allowed Taliesin to review his memories of the past few hours.

It seems your friends will be in need of future protection. I will bring some possibilities.

Renzo turned to prepare the others for Taliesin's imminent arrival, only to find the *Old One* standing in the center of the room.

"Greetings, Lady Guinevere." Taliesin gave Gwen a courtly bow before turning to Renzo. "Lord Lorenzo, if you would be so kind as to make me known to your guests?"

David was on his feet, standing between Taliesin and Rachel. If he'd owned a sword, Renzo felt sure he'd have drawn it.

Rachel peered around her fiancé, studying Taliesin with wide-eyed wonder.

"You are too quick for me, milord." Renzo grinned as he strode to Taliesin with open arms. "I was just about to let them know you were expected." After clasping outstretched hands with his fellow *Old One*, Renzo turned to make the introductions.

"David, Rachel, allow me to present Taliesin— an *Old One* and an extraordinary bard."

David relaxed his stance and stepped forward to shake Taliesin's hand.

Rachel stood and, looking a little uncertain, inclined her head.

"Taliesin, this is David Milligan and his newly espoused wife, Rachel Carson."

"Lorenzo has told me of your recent trials, Mr. Milligan. Please allow me to congratulate you on your good fortune in having such a devoted young woman's love."

"To what do we owe this pleasure, Lord Taliesin?" Gwen came forward at last and greeted Taliesin with a warm embrace.

"I am here to deliver the crystal vial I spoke to you about at Samhain." He produced a small item from his pocket and placed it in Gwen's hand.

A faceted gem about an inch long and a quarter inch in diameter, with a stopper so cleverly concealed that it took a moment's scrutiny for Renzo and Gwen to discover the opening. The crystal was banded in the center by finely wrought gold filigree which would allow the vial to be worn as a pendant on a chain. Examining the filigree more closely, the pair discovered that tiny sigils had been worked into the design.

Taliesin waited while Renzo and Gwen studied the jewel. When Gwen raised her eyes to his, he supplied the required instruction.

"After the blood has been obtained, seal the vial with the sigils inscribed in the filigree. As long as he wears it on his body, he will be free of Lilith's control. Warn him, though. He must never take it off. He should even leave instructions that it remain on his body after his death. He would not wish to give her the chance to reanimate his corpse."

Gwen shuddered.

Renzo took the vial from her trembling fingers and placed it on a chain around his neck. "Thank you, Taliesin," he said, "we will look for an opportunity to activate this charm."

Suddenly remembering her duties as hostess, Gwen exclaimed, "Forgive me, Lord. I haven't offered you a chair or refreshment. Please, be seated. May I bring you something to eat or drink?"

Taliesin smiled and, folding his long legs, settled himself into a chair directly across from the couch where David and Rachel sat.

"Thank you, Lady Guinevere, but I am in no need of refreshment." He waited until Renzo and Gwen were seated before making his next point. "I believe that you are concerned about protecting this young couple from further interference from Lilith?"

David's eyes narrowed, and Rachel's face paled. The subject hadn't come up. So much had happened in the last few hours...

the friends hadn't discussed whether or not the human couple might still be in danger.

"You think she'll try again?" David searched Renzo's face, his gaze intense and fierce.

"I do." Renzo met his stare with equal intensity. "You and Rachel are important to Gwen— and to me. That makes you targets. I was remiss in not seeking protection for you earlier." He glanced at Rachel. "I hope you'll both forgive me."

David barked— a harsh imitation of laughter. "Considering I'd still be locked in hell except for your efforts, I think forgiveness is a moot point. You're sorry. I'm grateful. Let's call it even and get on with life."

He reached across the intervening space and grasped Renzo's hand. "Friends?"

"Friends." Renzo affirmed, relief softening his expression. "Now, as to protection... what do you have in mind, Taliesin?"

"I would recommend a charm. Something to be worn on the body; never to be removed. We can make it a pendant, a ring, even a form of the body piercing which seems so popular among young mortals these days. The physical manifestation is irrelevant, whatever David and Rachel choose will be fine. What is important is the magical content."

Taliesin stopped to consider, studying Gwen. "I believe you hold the answer to this particular puzzle, Lady."

"Me?" Gwen's question reverberated like a gunshot in the quiet room. "I don't know anything about protective charms. Well, I mean, I read about them in the Gramarye, but I haven't had any practical experience with them."

"Haven't you? Think again, Lady."

"Oh. Well, yes, Merlin and Dylan and Mei have used a couple on me," Gwen's face mirrored her confusion, "but those were against mortal interference. That's not what we need here."

Renzo put an arm around her as he said, "I think he's referring to the sigil High Magic gave you. The newest, most potent sigil against magical interference."

"Very good, Lorenzo. Yes. That is the one I have in mind. I propose that we weave that sigil, along with samples of their DNA, into charms to be worn at all times."

"Why our DNA? And what kind of sample?" David was wary of any magic touching his body. Even benign magic designed to protect him.

"If I fashion a ring for you, for example, and place your DNA in the sigil it does two things. First, it makes the ring respond to your physical being: it will never be too tight or too loose. It will be incapable of falling off by accident. You would have to remove it by an act of will— and the sigil would protect you from magical interference with that choice. Secondly, it will deepen the power of the sigil, allowing it to know specifically who is to be protected from said interference."

Taliesin paused, regarding Gwen with his sea green eyes. "I cannot know for certain, but I believe High Magic sealed its charm to you in such fashion. High Magic has no need of your cooperation to sample your DNA. That ability is well within its sphere of influence."

Gwen fingered the tiny golden sigil dangling from her bracelet. "I don't know about that, but I do know I've never taken it off. It's never even occurred to me to take it off."

"Exactly." Taliesin returned his attention to David. "That is why I wish to weave your DNA into the charm. So that it will never even occur to you to remove the charm."

"Got it. That makes complete sense." David leaned forward, his expression challenging the elder *Old One*. "You didn't answer my second question. What kind of sample are we talking about?"

The bard laughed. The sound was bright with delight, immediately lifting the air of tension that had pervaded the room since Taliesin's introduction of the crystal vial.

The release was visible in the lines of their bodies; the tautness with which they held themselves relaxed.

"You are truly a man to be reckoned with, David Milligan." The smile remained on his face, inspiring further confidence in his mortal listeners. "You need not fear the sample. I'm talking about a strand of hair, or a nail clipping. We will spill no blood in Lady Guinevere's living room."

"Great. Let's get on with it." David turned his attention to Rachel. "What do you want? A ring? A necklace? An eyebrow stud?"

"I think I'd like a ring." She poked David in the chest with her index finger, eyes sparkling. "But this in no way removes your obligation to put a wedding ring on my left hand."

David looked shocked. "Didn't even occur to me that it might. Hell, I won't even try to get away with considering it an engagement ring." He gave Taliesin a roguish grin. "But I bet our friend here could make it look like one."

"Indeed, I could. But I will not." He smiled at the young couple. "You must fulfill your societal responsibilities on your own."

CHAPTER 34

"It was heaven, being back on the ranch." Gwen unpacked her suitcase while Rachel sat on the bed flipping through the pages of a bridal magazine.

"What did your aunt and uncle think of Renzo?"

Rachel was curious about how Renzo's reception had stacked up to the one David received at the Carson household. Of course, Renzo hadn't broken Gwen's heart a few weeks earlier. Rachel supposed her parents were allowed a certain wariness when it came to David Milligan.

"Oh, Aunt Katie loved him. Uncle Jem liked him, too, but you know how men are. He had to do a certain amount of poking and prodding, just to make sure Renzo was up to snuff." Gwen dropped the jeans she was folding and sat next to Rachel. "Do you know what? He even had the nerve to corner Renzo and ask him about his intentions. I don't know what got into him." She shook her head in amazement.

Rachel giggled at the thought of Gwen's cowboy uncle staring down the centuries-old *Old One*. Her dad didn't know how lucky he was.

"That must have been quite a scene. But, you have to be fair. Your uncle hasn't got a clue who, or what, Renzo is— bet you didn't tell them how he saved your life. Your uncle's just trying to protect his little girl." Rachel sighed and closed the magazine. "All in all, it sounds like Renzo got a much warmer reception than David did."

"Don't worry, Rach. David'll wear them down." Gwen patted Rachel's knee before jumping up to continue unpacking. "We all love him, and we were pretty aggravated with him a couple of weeks ago, too."

Just then the object of their discussion poked his head around the door frame. "Come on, you two. You can finish that later. The pizza's here, and I'm starved."

David pulled a long, forlorn face, and ducked when Rachel threw a pillow at him.

"Hey, no fair attacking the messenger. Seriously, Renzo won't let me touch the food 'til you guys are out there."

This last information, delivered in a pitiful whine, elicited a storm of giggles.

David withdrew, rolling his eyes at the cruelty of his fate. He was starving and they were laughing.

Women.

A few minutes later, the four friends sat in the living room eating pizza and drinking beer. At least, three of them were eating. David could more accurately be described as annihilating his food.

"What? Didn't you eat while we were in Colorado?" Renzo shook his head as David launched into his fourth large piece. No one else had even started their second.

"Hey, this marriage thing has me jittery. Nervous energy burns a lot of calories." He grinned at Rachel and bestowed a sloppy kiss on her cheek that had her scrambling for a napkin.

"Speaking of wedding stuff, you want to come ring shopping with me? You're going to need one, too, you know."

He was focused on his next bite of pizza, so it took him a minute to notice that everyone else had frozen.

"What?" David glanced from face to face. "Oh, give me a break. You mean you haven't asked her yet?" He stared at Renzo in amazed disgust.

"Come on, man. Everyone knows you two are a unit."

"David," Rachel hissed, urgently poking him in the ribs. "Shut up. You're out of line."

"No. It's okay, Rachel." Renzo turned to Gwen, his eyes shining with mirth. "This isn't very romantic, but do you want to get married? I was planning to wait for Beltane, ask Merlin to bind us in the *Old One* ritual, but if you'd like a mortal ceremony, we can do that too."

Gwen gazed deep into Renzo's eyes, allowed a thought tendril to caress his mind, and turned to glare at David. "You, David Milligan, are an unmitigated idiot."

David turned scarlet, opened his mouth to speak, then clamped it shut again.

Gwen allowed her expression to soften as she reached across the coffee table to touch his hand. "But I love you, anyway."

Turning her attention back to Renzo, she said, "If you wouldn't mind, I'd love a normal wedding. Aunt Katie and Uncle Jem can't come to the Beltane festival, and they'd be miserable if I just called and told them we're married."

"Of course. It's been so long since I've had a mortal family, I've forgotten about such considerations. Guinevere Enid Vaughan, will you be my wife? In the mortal realm as well as the *Old One*?"

"I will."

Renzo and Gwen kissed tenderly, then turned to smile at Rachel and David.

"This is so exciting." Rachel's eyes sparkled as she bounded off the couch to hug Gwen. "I have the most brilliant idea." Clasping Gwen's hands tightly, she smiled broadly at Renzo and David. "Why don't we make it a double wedding? It'll be twice as much fun, and half as much work!"

Gwen's mouth dropped open as she stared wild-eyed from Rachel to Renzo and back again. Closing her jaw with a snap, she studied her friend's face.

"Are you sure about this? I mean, do you really want to share such a special moment? What about David?"

"What about me?" David asked, genuinely surprised to hear his name mentioned.

"You wouldn't mind a double wedding, would you, David?"

He met Rachel's glowing eyes and answered with absolute sincerity. "Honey, we can get married underwater in a hurricane. Whatever you want. I just want you for my very own... permanently."

"Truly, Gwen, I think it would be fabulous to share our wedding day. It kind of makes up for all the things we didn't get to share growing up."

Gwen turned a questioning gaze on Renzo.

"It's up to you, my love," Renzo said with a silly grin. "For once, I agree wholeheartedly with David."

Gwen hugged Rachel tightly. "This is the best idea you've ever had. It'll be a wonderful day. After all, we were all together when the decisions were made— we just as well be together when the vows are taken."

"All righty. Now that all these little details are settled, how about we get back to my original question? You want to go ring shopping with me, Renzo?"

David threw an arm across his face to ward off Rachel's playful blow, while Renzo laughed heartily.

CHAPTER 35

"*O*h, Gwen. I'm so excited for you." Gwen heard the tears in Aunt Katie's voice as she listened to the exciting news. "Of course we'll come, but when? You haven't given me a date?"

"Oh. Right. New Year's Day. We're all getting married on New Year's Day. Can you think of a more perfect time?" Gwen's happy laughter rang through the apartment.

"Good Lord, child. That's less than a month away. How on earth will we get everything done?"

"Don't worry about a thing, Aunt Katie. Rachel's mom is the queen of organization when it comes to social events. She's arranging everything. All you need to do is show up with Uncle Jem in tow… and force him into nice clothes."

"Well, I can certainly manage that much. When should we plan to arrive?"

Gwen paused to catch her breath. She was so happy and excited that her hands were shaking as she held the phone to her ear. Everything was going so perfectly.

"Renzo and I were hoping you would come out for Christmas and stay through for the wedding. That is, if you can get away from the ranch that long. What do you think?"

"Oh, Gwen, this is a once in a life-time experience. We'll make it work." Katie's voice was thick with pride and determination. "Jem and I wouldn't miss this for the world. We'll see you at Christmas, then. I love you, sweetheart."

"I love you, too, Aunt Katie. Be sure to give Uncle Jem a big hug for me."

Tears of happiness stung Gwen's eyes as she ended the call. She was getting married in less than a month!

Talk about a whirlwind, but then the entire last year of her life had been one giant adventure. Might as well start the next one off with a bang.

Before she managed to move away, the phone rang. She answered, and found Rachel on the other end.

"Listen, Gwen, I know you're getting ready to go into finals next week, but do you think we could go shopping for our wedding dresses this weekend? Mom's been after me, and she's absolutely right— we have to get them ordered so they'll have time to get them in and have any alterations done."

Gwen felt breathless just listening to Rachel.

"Whoa, girl. Slow down. Yes, you're right, but should we wait for the weekend? Why not just go tomorrow after class?"

"Trust me, this will be an all day affair. I'll call the bridal shop— Mom knows the best one— and schedule an appointment. Mom will come with me, of course. It's too bad Katie can't be here to help you. Oh well, Mom thrives on this sort of thing. She'll just have to help both of us."

"We'll need help?" Gwen's voice squeaked at the ridiculous suggestion that she would need assistance trying on a few dresses.

Rachel laughed at Gwen's naivete. "You've got no clue. I went with my cousin to pick out her dress last year. We were totally exhausted by the end of the day. Happy, but exhausted."

"Whatever you say. You're obviously the expert. Okay, I've got Saturday all blocked out on my calendar." Gwen circled the day on her planner, mentally rearranging her study plans. "And you can let your mom off the hook. I'll see if Mei can come with us. She's my *Old One* mentor. You'll love her."

On Saturday Gwen discovered that Rachel had been absolutely correct. Shopping for the perfect gown was a marathon event.

Once the introductions were out of the way, Carly, their own personal clerk, showed the girls and their helpers to the fitting salon. Gwen had to stifle her amazement, she'd never imagined such places existed.

Each bride was given her own dressing room, complete with three-way mirrors, dais and a comfortable couch and chairs. Gwen's dressing room was easily as big as her bedroom. The two dressing rooms flanked an open display area lined with mirrors. There was a platform in front of the mirrors big enough to walk around on. Rachel quietly informed Gwen that it was for inspecting trains, to see that they moved appropriately when the bride walked.

Gwen shook her head in amazement as Carly led them to the showroom and pulled gown after gown out for their inspection;

frothy confections spun of sugar and dreams as well as elegant designs that wouldn't be out of place at a royal ball. Gwen was totally baffled. How could anyone make a choice? She watched with an awed combination of terror and pride as Rachel calmly directed Carly. Yes, she'd try that one. No, that was too over the top. This one? Well, perhaps.

Okay, if Rachel can do this, so can I. Gwen took a deep breath to calm the butterflies in their desperate attempt to escape her stomach.

Indeed, little sister. These are only dresses. Mei's mindspeech was soothing and calm. *Which ones please your eye? Simple lines, or the more ornate? You may try them all if you wish. It is your right, and the reason you are here.* Mei smiled into Gwen's eyes and squeezed her hand.

Accepting her mentor's transfusion of serenity and courage, Gwen smiled and asked Carly to show her that last dress again.

After each young woman had chosen several gowns, the real work began.

Now Gwen understood why Rachel had said she'd need an assistant. The gowns weighed a ton. It wasn't a simple matter of slipping a dress over her head, giving it a little tug and then stepping to the mirror to check the effect.

Oh no. First there were the daunting undergarments to be donned, and then there were gowns to be lifted above her head and dropped carefully into place. Mountains of satins, silks, laces and brocades. By the end of the morning the attendants' arms ached from the unaccustomed exercise, and Rachel and Gwen were exhausted from the effort required to move in gowns that fought to remain stationary.

Gwen reclined on the couch in her dressing room, enjoying a moment's peace. The room was littered with exquisite gowns; some hanging, some lying on the pristine floor waiting to be rehung. One stood in the middle of the dais, where she had managed to step out of it before falling on the couch. It seemed to have a life of its own; standing serenely in place, enticing her to make it her choice.

The door opened and Rachel stepped through wearing a robe provided by the salon. She dropped into the chair next to Gwen's feet and sighed. "Well, what do you think? Have you found the right one yet?"

Gwen raised her head and scanned the room. "I don't know. There are about four that look really good on me, but none of them stands out above the others. What about you? Have you made a decision?"

The long, slow smile that spread across Rachel's lips as well as the lustrous gleam in her eyes answered the question before she could frame the words. "Oh, yes. The velvet bodice with the brocade skirt. It's just what I've always dreamed of."

Nodding her head, Gwen pictured the gown Rachel described. "Yes. You were stunning in that one. You were the focus in that dress. It didn't wear you. I mean, some of these gowns— they just overwhelm you. It's like you're just there to show them off."

The girls were giggling as Mei joined them. She looked speculatively at Gwen. "Any decision yet?"

When Gwen shook her head, Mei smiled a slow, secret smile. "How do you feel about trying one more?" At Gwen's surprised expression, Mei nodded tranquilly. "I didn't want to interfere with your process, but as you've not made a choice... would you like to see an *Old One* gown?"

Rachel jumped up and ran to close the door. "It doesn't lock." She turned to look at Mei in alarm. "How will we explain a magic gown to Mother and Carly?"

Mei's laughter was liquid silver, cooling and refreshing their frazzled nerves. "Don't be concerned, little friend. Elizabeth and Carly are deep in discussion of veils and undergarments. They will remain so occupied until I give them leave to return to us."

She turned to Gwen and held out her hand. "Come, my lady."

Gwen rose, feeling very foolish at the formality in Mei's voice considering Gwen was in her underwear. She stepped onto the dais and studied Mei's reflection in the mirror before her.

Mei sketched a sigil in the air and Gwen was bathed in light. When the illumination vanished, Gwen heard Rachel gasp. Slowly, she turned her head to survey her own reflection.

Yes.

This was her wedding gown.

∿

RACHEL WAS STUNNED.

She'd never seen Gwen look so beautiful, so... regal. If she didn't know the vision on the dais was her childhood friend, she'd think she was looking at a young goddess.

Gwen stood arrayed in a gown from another time, another place.

Rachel couldn't begin to guess at the shimmery fabric, white and silky, but not silk. The form-fitting gown flowed from a ballet neckline to Gwen's slender hips, where it widened and fell in soft, graceful folds to her feet. The train swept luxuriously behind her, elegant but not overdone. The sleeves, fitted to the elbow, widened, allowing the back edge to glide to the floor. A delicate embroidery of silver lace formed a wide band around the neckline, while a girdle of silver filigree lightly encircled her hips.

An echo of that filigree adorned Gwen's head. The intricate headdress, dripping with seed pearls and crystals, sparkled against her dark hair like moonlight on water.

"It's magnificent, Mei." Rachel whispered, unwilling to break the reverent silence. "Gwen, you look... amazing."

Mei turned to Rachel, an expression of concern marring her features. "I'm sorry, Rachel. Would you like to try one as well? It wouldn't be identical to this, of course, but I know another that would suit you wonderfully."

Dragging her eyes away from Gwen, Rachel stared at Mei in surprise.

"What? Oh. No thank you, Mei." She laughed, a little self-consciously. "No, this is perfect for Gwen, but I don't need a gown spun from fairy dust. The one I've chosen is just what I've always dreamed of, but thank you for the offer."

She gave Mei a shy smile and then bounded to the dais to hug Gwen.

"It's going to be a perfect wedding!"

CHAPTER 36

Gwen stepped into the late afternoon sunshine and turned to look at the building she had just exited. "Can you believe it Renzo? My finals are finished; the term is over. The next time I enter that building, I'll be a married woman," she grabbed his hand and smiled up at him, "and my first quest will be successfully completed. I wonder what my next task will be?"

Laughing, Renzo drew her into the warmth of his embrace. "I can't answer that, my love." He dropped a kiss on the top of her head. "I applaud your optimism, but right now we need to concentrate on completing the current quest. We've barely got a week before Alban Arthuan. You need to find the clue."

Gwen hugged him tightly for a moment before stepping out of his embrace. "Don't worry, Renzo. I'm taking this sign seriously, and I know, because it's the last one, Lilith is likely to pull out the big guns." She took his hand again as they strolled across campus.

"We're as prepared as we know how to be. David and Rachel are protected, so are Katie and Jem. I'm protected from magical interference, and you and the others are working overtime to see that I'm safe from non-magic sources.

"We'll find the clue and we'll find the sign... and then we'll discover what this new sigil means."

They walked in companionable silence, enjoying the mild winter afternoon. Gwen, accustomed as she was to the harsher climate of the Colorado Rockies, had trouble remembering it was winter. The grass was green and hardy little pansies still bloomed in bright patches around the park. The temperatures were mild, and though it was often overcast and rainy, it hardly qualified as "winter" in her mind.

As they walked, Gwen contemplated the strangeness of this past year. She would be twenty-three years old next week. A year ago at this time, she'd never heard of Alban Arthuan. Now she knew that her birthday fell on that ancient holy day. Oh, she'd known she was a winter solstice baby; that had come up in school the year they studied rudimentary astronomy. She also knew that some cultures celebrated Yule on or about her birthday, but the Celtic term *Alban Arthuan* had never come up.

How strange. A year ago today, she hadn't known she was an *Old One*; had not had a clue that magic was real, and that she could manipulate it.

What a bizarre and wonderful year it had been. Her quest had taken her to so many fascinating places. She hadn't spent much time in any of those exotic locales, but still, she, Guinevere Enid Vaughan, had set foot on six of the world's seven continents. And she'd be setting foot on the seventh on her twenty-third birthday.

Gwen stopped walking so suddenly that Renzo nearly tripped. He turned quickly to see her eyes widen, her mouth open in a little "O" of surprise.

"What is it? Gwen? Are you all right?"

She cocked her head slightly, to bring him into focus. Closed her mouth, then threw herself into his arms with a squeal of delight.

"I don't need a clue." Gwen jumped back from his surprised embrace and did a little happy-dance on the sidewalk. "I don't need a clue. I already know where to find the final sign."

Renzo grabbed her by the shoulders and held her in place.

"Where? How? Stop dancing and explain."

With a final energetic twirl, Gwen stood still, eyes shining with excitement. "Think Renzo. There are seven signs; to be found on seven of the eight Arcane High Days; one on each of..."

"The seven continents." he finished for her. "Of course. The final sign is on the only continent you haven't searched. Antarctica."

"I don't need more direction than that. I just need to know which part of the world to concentrate on... my power will do the rest. There is no clue to decipher this time. Oh, Renzo... we're almost done."

"Congratulations, my love. You're ready. Now we just have to wait for the solstice." Renzo kissed her, felt his blood begin to sizzle, and hugged her tightly. He separated from her with difficulty, and said in a husky, strained voice, "Let's go home and celebrate."

The expression in his eyes sent waves of delight surging through Gwen's body; she glowed with blissful anticipation.

"I can't think of anything I'd rather do."

CHAPTER 37

$\mathcal{L}$ ilith stormed through her palace in a frenzy of rage. Nothing she had done had stopped that beastly little ignoramus. Only one sign remained. Alban Arthuan would be her last opportunity to prevent High Magic from forming its new sigil. She'd been around long enough to understand that if the sigil took this much effort to form, it would be a powerful weapon for the Light. And the last thing she wanted was to face a powerful new weapon. The sigil had to be destroyed before it could be formed.

But so far, all her attempts had failed.

Oh, how it rankled that she, the Queen of Darkness, had no idea how Gwen had freed David Milligan. Lilith had been certain he was firmly under her control, beyond Gwen's ability to redeem. Not in the manner she would have preferred, of course. If she had managed to seduce him, she could have used him very effectively to neutralize Gwen— and that besotted fool, Lorenzo Santini.

How could *Old Ones* be so stupid as to trust mortals with their secrets?

She would have enjoyed using David to kill Gwen, and then bring the distraught Renzo to her. Unfortunately, that hadn't worked out. The insipid mortal had proved stronger than her seductive wiles. But still, she had removed him from the playing field very effectively.

The man should be buried alive by now, his friends and family mourning his death.

How had they freed him? It was unthinkable, that she should be continually bested by that mortal-loving infant.

As Lilith paced back and forth in her cold bedchamber, she scrutinized the information she possessed regarding Gwen's defenses.

The girl wore High Magic's blasted protective sigil. The Dark *Old Ones* could not directly attack her with magic. Samuel had tested that theory and forfeited his life.

Mortal violence worked very effectively against the little snot. Oh, that had been a glorious evening. Lilith reveled momentarily in the remembrance of Gwen's pain and anguish... but Santini had ended her pleasure before it had truly begun.

Lilith recognized with defeat that her subsequent attempts to use mortals against Gwen had proved useless. The girl was simply too well guarded. There was never a moment that her watchdog *Old One* or that idiot mortal weren't on guard.

Her defenses were even more impenetrable when she sought for the signs. Then she was accompanied by an honor guard of *Old Ones* who held the wards at all four compass points.

The situation had become altogether too distressing. The little chit already had six of the seven signs in her possession. Her quest had taken her to six of the seven continents of the world.

Lilith understood the significance.

If all the continents were represented, as well as all the elements, the sigil would be a force she did not want to reckon with.

Wait a minute!

Lilith's eyes widened, cracking the cruel mask of anger that weighed heavily upon her face. Her features, revealed by the unrestrained wonder shining from her eyes, illustrated the pure beauty that had once graced her soul, as well as her face.

But the mask of cruelty and distemper clamped back in place before the infinitesimal slip could be noticed... had there been anyone present to see.

The chit had found six signs, one each on six of the seven continents. Her search would bring her into Lilith's domain next. And on the longest night of the year... the pinnacle of the Dark's strength.

Think!

There must be a weakness in the Light's defense. There had to be a chink in their armor. Her honor guard couldn't protect her every minute.

Her honor guard...

Yes! There was their Achilles heel.

Oh, this was going to be rich.

A chilling cackle burst from her throat as Lilith strode to her assembly hall. Once there, she called her cadre of Dark *Old Ones*.

They were a damned lot.

Old Ones born to the noble purposes of High Magic, but with flawed souls. For these *Old Ones* had sacrificed their birthright to the dark god of unrestrained power; had made their choice, and sealed their doom in Lilith's arms. An act of betrayal all the more damning because each had gone to her knowing the evil she embodied. These were not innocent mortals, unschooled in the wiles of magic, but powerful sorcerers who willingly embraced their fate.

Lilith smiled at her consorts— male *Old Ones* tied to her by desire and a corruption of ancient magic. The darkness of their souls fed by the inky pools of degraded underworld power that surrounded her chosen fortress.

Lilith's body was their temple. Her womb the altar into which they poured their sacrificial seed. Sacrifices willingly made to gain strength from those pools of limitless power.

They had no wish to be constrained by the Light, and so they were damned by the dark.

"Make ready for battle, my warriors." Lilith's voice rang out cold and clear.

All who heard it gloried in the triumphant tones of her terrible joy.

"The Light will bring the battle to us; we need not seek them out. Rejoice, for I have found the chink in their armor. We will prevail."

CHAPTER 38

*G*wen stretched luxuriously and reached for Renzo. Her searching fingers found nothing but sheets and blankets, the creases where he had lain. Opening her eyes, she drank in the bright sunshine sparkling around her bed.

What a gift, after all the cloudy days we've had.

Gift...

Gwen lurched out of bed and danced around the room.

Happy Birthday to me! It's my birthday, and my first gift is sunshine spilling through my windows. It's going to be a glorious day.

Anxious to join Renzo in the kitchen, Gwen hurried through her early morning bathroom rituals. His voice carried lightly through the apartment, singing as he cooked. Gwen's nostrils flared, savoring the rich scents of coffee and frying bacon, along with the sweet overtones of cinnamon and nutmeg.

When she was brushed, combed and warmly wrapped in a fluffy robe, Gwen waltzed into the kitchen.

"Good morning, Lorenzo Alan Santini."

Renzo whirled to face her, eyes sparkling, a mug of coffee in one hand. He presented the mug with a flourish. "Good morning, Guinevere Enid Vaughan— soon to be Santini." He bestowed a gentle kiss on Gwen's forehead. "Blessings on this special day."

Gwen laughed and accepted the mug of coffee. "Mmm. Everything smells wonderful. When do we eat?"

"Be seated, my lady, for breakfast is served." Renzo assembled a plate for his lady love. Scrambled eggs, crisp bacon and two perfectly browned cinnamon walnut pancakes. It was more than she was likely to eat, but this was a special occasion.

"I would have brought you breakfast in bed, but you're too fast for me."

"And don't you forget it, my fine handsome man." Gwen choked out a laugh at the bemused expression on Renzo's face. "This is wonderful, Renzo. Beautiful sunlight and a delicious feast. What more could a girl want on her twenty-third birthday?"

Renzo sat down across from her as he reached into his pocket. "Well, I'm hoping you'll want this as well."

He placed a small velvet box on the table by her coffee, then lifted the lid to reveal a sparkling diamond solitaire.

Gwen nearly choked on the forkful of eggs she had just put in her mouth. She grabbed her napkin, coughing and wheezing, while tears gathered in her eyes. Renzo was around the table in a flash, trying to slap her on the back and hug her at the same time, until she held up her hand to stop his efforts.

"I'm fine." she gasped, trying desperately to control the giggles that threatened to explode once she had the breath to expend. "Really, Renzo, I'm just fine now."

He laid his head on her shoulder and exhaled a shuddering breath. "This isn't at all how I imagined it."

When he heard her giggle, he rocked back on his heels and grinned at her. "I really wasn't trying to kill you with my engagement ring." They both laughed, enjoying the moment.

When their mirth was under control, Renzo returned to his chair, watching in satisfaction as Gwen took the ring from the box and placed it on her finger. She studied the sparkling solitaire before raising equally sparkling eyes to his.

"It's perfect, Renzo. Thank you."

Reaching across the table with her bejeweled hand, she clasped his.

"Now it's perfect," he whispered, raising her hand to his lips, "now that it's on your finger."

They gazed into each other's eyes, breakfast forgotten, until the timer on the oven shrilled.

Renzo startled. "Drat! I forgot about the muffins."

Sprinting to the kitchen, he pulled a pan her favorite blueberry muffins from the oven.

Seriously, this man of hers was too good to be true! Grinning and shaking her head to clear the cobwebs, Gwen took another cautious bite of her birthday breakfast.

Honestly... how many women received diamonds with their bacon and eggs?

CHAPTER 39

*J*ust before dusk Merlin, Mei, and Dylan arrived to guard Gwen on her seventh and final search. Each *Old One* was formally dressed in silver robes, and each carried his or her staff. While the other three chatted, Merlin drew Gwen aside.

"I want you to remember, Guinevere, there is special power in the anniversary of an *Old One's* birth. Not only is this Alban Arthuan, it is also *your* day. If we encounter more resistance than we expect, don't be afraid to draw on that power."

The ancient *Old One* smiled at her, but it was a smile of determination and resolve, not of joy.

"This celebration of the longest night of the year is the Arcane High Day that lends itself most easily to manipulation by the dark powers. I don't think it's an accident that it's also the day of your birth; the extra strength gained from that anniversary may be our saving grace."

Gwen nodded, feeling a little weak in the knees, uncertain whether or not her voice would actually produce words.

Merlin smiled, and this time his eyes lit as well.

"Blessings upon you, Lady. You have accomplished much in your first year among us. You make us all proud."

So saying, he took Gwen by the hand and led her to the circle of her friends, her people.

"Come. The time is upon us. The threshold of not-day-not-night waits to be crossed. The longest night of the year is straining to be born. We shall emerge in strengthening Light in the morning. Tomorrow begins the growth of Light, the waning of Dark.

"But that is tomorrow; tonight there is a quest to complete."

Gwen stood straight and still as her four *Old One* guards took up their stations at the compass points around her.

Merlin raised his staff, looked each of them in the eye and said, "Blessings of strength and Light upon you. Lady Guinevere, you may begin."

Gwen twisted Renzo's ring on her finger and sought the assurance of his gaze. They locked gazes; he smiled and nodded, and Gwen gathered her courage and stepped into the gelatinous bubble of her strength, her power, her destiny.

Swinging her consciousness to the far south, Gwen sought the glimmer of the final sign on the ice-choked continent of Antarctica. Distance fell away as her soul soared toward the final piece of this year-long puzzle.

She was no longer the frightened girl who had been pulled into this bubble unknowing a year ago. She had accepted her *Old One* heritage with pride, and in doing so had found her center— the undying love of the man who was her equal, her mate.

She and Renzo would sail the centuries together— as effortlessly as her power now sailed the globe.

There!

The glimmer of golden light revealed itself to her questing mind.

There!

Gwen gathered the lines of power, grasped the tendrils of her guardians' thoughts firmly, and threw them all into the abyss…

…emerging effortlessly on the other side.

If her emergence was effortless, it was also unexpected.

Gwen did not find herself standing a few feet from the pulsating glow of the final sign. Nor did she find herself encircled by her friends.

She was alone, in a cold, sterile white room. Not an ice cave or crevasse, but a room of unrelieved, glaring whiteness. She whirled in a circle, unable to fathom what had gone wrong.

Seeking information, she extended her senses.

Nothing.

No sound reached her ears, no scent enticed her nostrils, and her head throbbed from the visual overload of the unrelieved whiteness surrounding her. Closing her eyes, she traced the mind-speech sigil in the air and sought her friends. A thick gray fog enveloped her thought tendril. Ignoring its cloying stickiness, Gwen pushed on.

They existed.

Renzo, Merlin, Dylan, Mei.

She chanted their names, a mantra of remembrance.

She could not, *would not* allow the pool of inky vileness to pull them from her thoughts.

Understanding clicked in her consciousness, and Gwen snapped back to herself.

A pool of inky vileness.

They had emerged near a fissure.

Quickly she sketched the now familiar wards against that foulness and initiated the mindspeech sigil again. This time she found Merlin at once.

But Merlin was besieged.

He couldn't spare the energy to converse with Gwen. With a flick of his mind, he opened his sight to her... he, Dylan and Mei were in a desperate battle with a host of Dark *Old Ones*.

Gwen's instinct was to join their fight.

No. Merlin's mindvoice was ragged. *Find the sign.* He used what energy he could spare to throw her from his mind.

Her eyes flew open as realization struck.

Renzo.

Renzo had not been with the other *Old Ones*.

Gwen had not found his mind when she searched, had found Merlin instead. Yet Renzo should've been the first mind she touched... he was the one she loved.

No!

Her mind reeled beneath the terrible realization. Why hadn't she seen it before?

Renzo was the flaw in their plan!

They had gone to great lengths to protect the mortals closest to her, to keep Lilith from gaining leverage over her by threats to their safety. But in their arrogance, they had done nothing to defend Renzo.

The man who held her heart in his hands.

Gwen shoved hysteria and desperation aside. He was here. She would find him. With the wards against the fissure in place, Gwen knew that she could do what needed to be done.

Find the sign...

Find her love...

Get them all out of whatever hell her quest had landed them in.

Holding her emotions tightly in check, Gwen stepped into her power again.

There.

The sign glimmered dully, grimed by a haze of darkness from the nearby fissure.

She threw herself toward it, and this time emerged within a few feet...

...but what occupied that short span of space stopped her cold.

Renzo's lifeless body sprawled before her, the sign pulsing dully between his left ear and the stark white wall.

All breath left Gwen's body, leaving her feeling cold and lifeless. If he were dead... he couldn't be dead. She couldn't live without him, but she was standing here, her heart beating dully in her chest. He had to be alive.

"So, you've finally found your man."

Gwen forced her eyes away from the man she loved, recovering herself enough to focus on Lilith who sat a few yards away on a magnificent marble throne. The Dark *Old One* gave no indication that she was aware of the sign's existence, but Renzo's body shielded it from her view... and its glimmer was very dim.

"You have no power over me, Lilith."

The knowledge was small comfort. Not if she had lost Renzo. Gwen sealed the pain in a corner of her mind. She had to remain alert in the other woman's presence.

"True." Lilith preened, enjoying this turn of events. "But I don't need to harm you... not while he lives." She nodded in Renzo's direction.

A rush of hope flooded Gwen's soul.

"Of course, he won't live long," Lilith said, a malicious gleam in her eyes. "Not if you don't hand that bracelet over to me at once."

Thoughts racing, Gwen turned her attention fully to Lilith. The signs were vulnerable to Lilith's power until they were formed into one sigil by the acquisition of the final piece.

If Gwen handed them over, Lilith would destroy them.

If Gwen held them back, Lilith would destroy Renzo.

The final sign was within her reach, but she didn't know if she could grab the sign and form the sigil in time to keep Renzo alive.

She had no way of knowing what the finished sigil's power would be. Even if she managed to bring it into being, she didn't know if it would be of any use in her present predicament.

Playing for time, Gwen glanced at Renzo's body, then spoke to Lilith.

"I need to know that the body I see is truly Renzo's. It could be nothing more than a cruel phantasm designed to intimidate me."

"Are your powers so weak?" Lilith's tone was incredulous, disparaging, but she waved a hand, giving Gwen what she needed — permission to approach Renzo's body.

He lay absolutely still. Even with death veiling his features, he was so incredibly handsome. Gwen drank in the sight of him, memorizing every detail of his beloved face.

David and Rachel would have to marry without them; but they would be able to marry because of Renzo and Gwen. Their life together would be a brief, but brilliant monument to Renzo and Gwen's love... a love that should have lasted through eternity.

Gwen jerked her thoughts away from that chasm; away from the grief that threatened to wipe all thought from her mind. She leaned forward to kiss her love farewell, and as she did, a single tear slid down her nose, and splashed on Renzo's cheek.

Using the gentle kiss as a distraction to Lilith's watchful eyes, Gwen placed her hand over the tiny glow beside Renzo's ear. Her fingers connected with the sign.

With a growl of rebellious pride, Gwen raised her head to Lilith and brought the seventh sign into contact with the other six.

"You may rob me of my love, my life and my destiny— but you will not rob High Magic of the product of my quest."

Lilith's shriek split the air as the room exploded in a raging inferno. Gwen tried desperately to shield Renzo's body, but as she scrambled for purchase on the suddenly twisting floor, she was startled into stillness.

Renzo rose from the floor, staff in hand.

Power and rage radiated from him in waves as he drove Lilith before him. As the dark sorceress scuttled away from his wrath, Lilith slipped and fell, cracking her skull on the marble dais.

Dazed by her injury and frightened by the maelstrom of power throbbing around her, Lilith huddled in a corner of the room, screams of terror and rage pouring from her mouth.

Before Gwen's shocked eyes, the self-proclaimed Queen of Darkness shriveled and bent into a wizened hag.

Renzo glowered at Lilith, disgust etched in every line of his face. Pointing his staff at the dais of her throne, he blasted the marble into small chunks. Bending down, he carefully plucked a single shard from the shattered ruins.

Turning, Renzo pulled Gwen to her feet, and without a word transported them back to the safety of their warded apartment.

But not before she heard a booming deep in the earth... a gathering rumble that signified the imminent collapse of Lilith's palace of ice.

CHAPTER 40

*W*hen Gwen and Renzo materialized in their living room, her first reaction was to throw her arms around his neck and never let him go again. Renzo, however, had other ideas. He pulled Gwen's arms roughly away from his neck and took her lips in a fiercely passionate kiss.

She was so dazed by the intensity of his caress, that it took a moment for her brain to reestablish contact with her body. At last, her senses cleared and she stepped away so she could look at him.

"You're alive. I didn't think either of us would get out of there alive— but certainly not you." She threw herself back into his arms. "What happened, Renzo? How did we get away?"

Renzo picked his trembling fiancee up, and carried her to the couch. Once he had seated himself and arranged Gwen comfortably on his lap, Renzo explained.

"You were absolutely amazing, Gwen. I can't tell you how proud I am of you, or how stupid I feel for letting myself get caught and putting you in that position."

His arms tightened around her body. Burying his face in her hair, he waited a beat before continuing.

"For right now, be content to know that you broke her spell, allowing me to free myself. I'd like to just sit here and hold you, but there are a couple of loose ends that require our immediate attention." Renzo breathed in the heady perfume that was uniquely Gwen and exhaled slowly. Very gently he placed her on the couch and stood.

"How can I help?"

"Call David. Have him swing by Whittier's home and pick him up. I need them both here as soon as possible." As he spoke, Renzo strode to the center of the room and placed wards around himself.

"I've got to find Dylan and the others."

He closed his eyes and formed the mindspeech sigil.

Gwen raced to the bedroom for her cell phone and placed a hurried call to David. By the time she explained what Renzo wanted and received David's assurance that he'd get right on it, Gwen could hear voices in her living room. She ran back to find Merlin, Dylan and Mei collapsed in comfortable chairs.

"Is everyone all right? Oh, I can't believe we all made it out."

Gwen's voice was so thick, she was afraid she might give in to wails of hysteria. Pushing her fist tightly to her mouth, she joined Renzo on the couch.

"Be at ease, Lady," Merlin said in a wheezing voice. "We have won the day. From the destruction we witnessed as we fled the palace, it will be quite some time before the Dark *Old Ones* trouble us further."

Renzo pulled Gwen into his embrace. "Is David coming? With Whittier?"

"Yes. He said he'd be here as soon as possible."

"If we have a few minutes, could someone please help me piece together what just happened?" Dylan looked weary beyond his long years, but his eyes shone with curiosity.

"I believe I can get the story started." Merlin sat up, rested his forearms on his knees, his hands dangling between them.

"Gwen's search took us into Lilith's palace. We hadn't anticipated being pulled into the heart of the largest fissure on the planet, so we were easily scattered by the magical fracturing of the dark pool. Before we could get our bearings, Dylan, Mei and I were attacked by the Dark *Old Ones*. The battle was intense, but we held them off."

He paused and studied Gwen's face. "It was very noble of you to want to come to our aid. I'm sorry I had to push you out of my mind, but I knew if you didn't complete your task, there might be no hope for us."

He closed his eyes and leaned back against the cushioned surface of the chair.

"I materialized right in front of Lilith's throne." Renzo picked up the thread of the tale, and supplied his own experience. "If I didn't know better, I'd say Lilith had directed me there. At any rate, she was prepared for me, but I wasn't prepared for her. She locked me in my body before I was even aware that the rest of you weren't with me."

He spoke directly to Gwen, now. "It was just like what she did to David. I could hear everything, but my hearing was the only sense I retained. I could feel her seal holding my power just beyond my reach. And then I heard your voice."

Renzo licked his lips and scanned the other *Old Ones*. "Gwen was incredible. You should have heard her, calmly challenging Lilith. Can you imagine? She even managed to finagle her way into touching my body."

He turned his eyes to Gwen's again. "That's what did it, you know. Just like what Rachel did for David."

"What?" Gwen looked genuinely puzzled. "I wasn't plotting anything clever. I was kissing you good-bye. I couldn't think of any way I was going to be able to complete the quest and protect you at the same time."

"But you did," he said quietly.

He glanced at the others, explaining, "It was the combination of her tears and her kiss that broke Lilith's seal." He watched as understanding dawned in the other *Old Ones'* eyes.

"With the seal broken, it only took me a few seconds to regain control of my power, but by that time, Gwen had completed the sigil and all hell had broken loose."

"Ahh, so that's what brought on the cataclysm," Dylan said, understanding coloring his voice. "The world falling apart around everyone's ears gave us our chance to escape from their overwhelming force."

"That's not the only thing that allowed you to escape." Renzo stood and walked to the hearth. He gazed at the painting of Haystack Rock that hung above the mantle for a moment, then turned to face his friends. "I was mad as hell when I got my control back. Ready to tear Lilith limb from limb. What happened to her was probably worse."

He returned to the couch and knelt before Gwen. "It happened so fast, I'm not sure you're aware. Look at your bracelet."

Gwen forced her attention from Renzo's face and raised her arm to display the varied charms.

They were gone.

Two things hung from her bracelet now.

Only two.

The protective sigil High Magic had given her early in her quest, and a medallion much too large to be worn on a bracelet.

The medallion was easily two inches across, made from an indescribable metal. The outer edge was a circle, which surrounded a very complex Celtic knot. The knotwork twisted and turned, luring her vision one way while the line went another. It would be very difficult, if not impossible, to trace this sigil. The unknown metal seemed to twist and writhe, as well, as if various parts of the knot were made of different substances... and the composition changed from moment to moment.

The medallion would have frightened her, except that it felt so right against her skin.

Her quest had created it; the medallion was hers.

Gwen was meant to carry this unchancy thing.

Pulling gaze eyes from the medallion, Gwen glanced at Renzo. "There's more. I can feel it. Tell us."

Renzo twisted around to sit beside Gwen again. He locked eyes with Merlin.

"That," he said indicating the medallion, "healed the fissure. It didn't just close it. It dried it up and removed it as if it had never been there."

Merlin nodded slowly. "That's how we escaped. They lost their power source. You mentioned Lilith. What happened to her?"

Gwen shivered. "She dried up, too." She raised her gaze to Merlin. "Renzo's right, it was awful. She shriveled up into this nasty wretch— like she was suddenly a thousand years old. She was screaming something awful when we left."

"You didn't actually see her die, then?" The soft query came from Mei. "I would not discount her ability to return if we have not cremated her lifeless husk."

Again, Merlin nodded. "You are wise, Lady Mei. But whether she lives, or died in the destruction of her palace, is of no consequence to us at this moment. If she lives, she will make herself known in due time. For now, let us enjoy our victory… and a season of peace."

Merlin, Dylan and Mei all rose, preparing to leave.

Renzo rose as well, and put a hand on Merlin's arm. "Please, Lord. I know you're tired, but there is one last matter on which I would appreciate your counsel."

Looking startled, Merlin resumed his seat. "Of course, Lorenzo. How may we be of service?"

Renzo remained standing and pulled a small ball of energy from the pocket of his silver robe. "When the cataclysm began, Lilith struck her head on the dais of her throne. The wound bled. Before we left, I shattered the marble and retrieved this shard. I encased it in an energy shield to preserve it. I have not touched the blood, only the end of the shard."

Gwen gasped, hardly daring to hope that what Renzo was suggesting might be true.

"My question is: will this blood suffice to work the charm that you and Taliesin described to me at Samhain? I have the crystal vial. Taliesin brought it to me a few weeks ago. The mortal,

Whittier, is on his way here. If I release the force field and allow him to collect the droplet, will the spell be complete?"

Merlin shook his head in amazement. "Lorenzo, you are a wonder. That you could think of such a thing at such a time... astounding.

"But I haven't answered your question. Yes. The plan you outline will meet all the requirements of the enchantment Taliesin and I debated at Samhain." His eyes twinkling merrily, Merlin shook Renzo's hand. "Congratulations, my lord. Very well done."

CHAPTER 41

*J*ason Whittier stood in the living room of his comfortable three bedroom home.

He was free.

He wiped the cold sweat from where it had formed on his brow. The nightmare was over. The crystal vial that hung around his neck felt warm against his skin. Never in his staid existence had he worn objects of personal adornment, but he blessed all that was good in the universe that this particular necklace existed.

He was free.

That evil witch, Lilith, would never touch his body or soul again. Never force him to do unthinkable acts; never cause him to think illogical, unsupported thoughts.

He still found it unbelievable, but after all the needlessly cruel things he had said to her, Miss Vaughan had been willing to help him; her friend and protector had devised a way to free him from Lilith's web.

Jason recognized that he was far from blameless in the course of events that had led to his entrapment. He should have been wiser — less susceptible to an aging, lonely man's fantasy of bedding an intoxicating young beauty.

Shaking his head in disbelief, Jason made a valiant attempt to acknowledge his own folly, to let the light of clarity shine on the events of the last six months. It would be far too easy to fall into the trap of rationalization, to allow himself to believe that he had been a hapless victim of an enchantress' wiles.

Indeed, he had been Lilith's victim, but he forced himself to admit the truth: he had made the process far too easy for her.

Striding purposefully to the gilt-framed mirror which hung above his mantle, Jason gazed deep into his own eyes.

"You've had a glimpse into your own soul, Jason Whittier, and found it wanting." A steely-eyed reflection glared back at him, defying him to weasel out of the truth. "Mr. Santini and Miss Vaughan have given you a second chance. See that you are worthy of it."

With that thought in mind, the venerable anthropology professor moved to his library and selected several reference volumes. Jason Whittier had spent his life studying the social interactions of humankind. He knew how to research. How hard could it be to discover the answers to the questions that burned in his soul?

What manner of creatures were Lilith... and Miss Vaughan and Mr. Santini?

Whatever they were, they weren't normal humans, of that Jason Whittier was certain.

CHAPTER 42

*G*wen stood in the wide lobby of Portland International Airport anxiously scanning faces in the horde of arriving passengers. Renzo sat at ease in a nearby chair, flipping idly through the pages of a glossy news magazine while he waited for Jem and Katie's arrival.

"Where are they? Their plane landed twenty minutes ago. We couldn't have missed them, could we?" Gwen's voice was tight with distress.

Renzo smothered a grin and stood to place an arm around her waist. "Relax, my love. It takes a while just to get off the plane. You know those lines always move at a snail's pace, with everyone yanking stuff out of the overhead bins. And once they finally get out of the plane it's a bit of a hike to get to the lobby."

He did smile now, and kissed the top of her head as well. "They can't get lost between the gate and the lobby."

Gwen had just begun to relax when he felt renewed tension telegraph itself from her waist to his arm. He looked up in time to see Jem and Katie stride around the corner, following the flow of people.

"Oh, there they are." Gwen jumped up and down, waving her hand frantically in the air. "Oh, Renzo. They're here."

He could tell she was restraining herself with difficulty. It was obviously hard to wait for them to clear the secured area before she pushed past other passengers to envelope her loved ones in a boisterous hug.

Renzo quickly stepped in to help Jem move the excited women to one side, out of the main flow of foot traffic.

"Look, Aunt Katie. Isn't it the most gorgeous ring you've ever seen?" Gwen's face glowed with happiness as she flashed the diamond solitaire for Katie's inspection.

Jem rolled his eyes and shrugged as he met Renzo's gaze. "Women. Honestly, can't this wait 'til we get to Gwen's place?"

He tried to sound gruff, but the smile tugging at his lips made it difficult. "Well, come on man. We can at least go collect the bags while they're blubbering."

Renzo laughed and clapped his soon-to-be uncle on the shoulder.

"Great idea. Baggage claim is this way." He pointed out their path and called over his shoulder to Gwen, "We'll see you down there in a few minutes. Don't get lost."

The wink that accompanied that last comment sent his keyed up fiancee into a fit of giggles.

Katie gave Gwen another exuberant hug, then stood back to look at her. "It seems like only yesterday we were retrieving you from the Denver airport— a woebegone little mite, if ever I saw one. And here you stand, a woman grown. About to be married."

She patted her niece's arm and bent to pick up her carry-on bag, but Gwen had already shouldered it. They linked arms and strolled toward baggage claim.

"It's been quite a year, Aunt Katie. I've grown up a lot." Gwen's forehead wrinkled in a slight frown as she thought of all the experiences that had been part of that growing that Katie would never know.

"I graduated from CU; moved to Portland; found my own apartment; began my grad work— and somewhere in there, found the time to meet Renzo and fall in love."

The frown was replaced with a sense of calm serenity. If she couldn't share everything that she was with Katie, she could certainly share the most important part. There was no need to conceal her deep love for Renzo.

"I'm so happy for you, honey. He seems to me to be a fine young man." They stopped a few paces away from where Jem and Renzo were collecting luggage. Katie watched her niece's chosen mate lift a suitcase from the conveyer belt.

"I'm looking forward to getting to know him better."

CHAPTER 43

The days between the Harrison's arrival and the New Year's Day wedding were filled with frantic activity. Katie and Jem had arrived on Christmas Eve day, so their initial time together was filled with the sights, sounds and scents of Christmas. The lack of snow, coupled with the jewel bright tones of the grass and persistent flowers, made it hard at first for the mountain dwellers to remember that the holiday was truly upon them. But the familiar sounds of carols and the wonderful display of holiday lights eased their transition.

Renzo and Gwen took them to a Christmas Eve service with Rachel's family. The beauty of the holy story filled them all with a sense of peace and reverence, setting the mood for the next day's festivities.

The day after Christmas, the serenity ended.

The week between Christmas and New Years was filled with fittings, flowers, and food. Last minute details like final head counts, and how many bottles of champagne and sparkling cider had to be dealt with.

Elizabeth Carson had arranged for the wedding to take place on an elegant commercial yacht. The ceremony, as well as the reception, would be held in the ballroom as the yacht swam majestically down the Willamette River. Elizabeth had outdone herself with the arrangements for decorations, buffet menu and two wedding cakes. The buffet was to be arranged in a horseshoe configuration, with a wedding cake at each end. Each bride and groom would cut their cake at the same moment.

Though Elizabeth had made all the arrangements, Gwen and Rachel had chosen the designs and flavors of their own cakes. Rachel's was to be three-tiered, poppy seed, with a very traditional look— complete with miniature bride and groom at the top. Gwen had opted for three tiers as well, but had asked that hers be iced smooth and decorated with fresh flowers, and since Renzo loved chocolate, that was her choice.

At last the big day arrived.

Renzo and David stood at the prow of the yacht on the highest enclosed level. The room was filled with white folding chairs set in neat rows, with an aisle down the center for the brides' entrance. The minister stood behind the men, and behind him was a wide window framing a stunning view of the Willamette River.

Renzo gazed anxiously down the aisle for his first sight of Gwen, who would be the first to come down the aisle. Rachel and Gwen had chosen not to have attendants; they agreed it would be cumbersome in a double wedding— especially in the confines of the yacht. Now the men waited, outwardly calm, but inwardly anxious to have the ceremony behind him.

JEM AND GWEN appeared at the back of the aisle. David was impressed. That gown really suited her. He was relieved to see that Jem was visibly nervous; seeming almost frightened to touch the vision who stood beside him. David watched as Gwen quickly scanned the room for familiar faces. He knew the moment her eyes found Renzo; saw the radiant smile bloom, recognized the love in her expression.

The love that banished all thought of nervousness from her mind.

RENZO SAW GWEN...

...and felt his heart drop to his toes.

Blessed be! Where had she found that gown?

She looked... she was...

...he had no words. He had no breath!

He'd always assumed that 'breathtaking' was simply an expression, but that was before he saw the woman he loved arrayed like a goddess on their wedding day.

She was quite simply breathtaking.

This vision— with her hair covered in moonbeams and dewdrops— loved him.

This powerful *Old One* was about to pledge to love him for eternity.

Why was he so blessed among men and *Old Ones*?

This mortal ceremony was a fine beginning, but Renzo could hardly wait for the ancient *Old One* rite that would take place at Beltane... for she was the center of his universe.

Renzo proudly accepted Gwen's hand as her uncle presented her to him.

. . .

DAVID PULLED his eyes away from the couple beside him and looked expectantly down the aisle. His time had arrived.

And there she was. His Rachel. His perfect, elegant, Rachel.

Gwen looked unearthly— like the creature of magic he knew her to be.

Rachel was... perfect. His down-to-earth, flesh-and-blood woman.

Who needed magic when he could hold Rachel in his arms?

David's proud smile broadened as he watched her approach him on her father's arm. The velvet and brocade, the lacy veil, the pearls at her throat... there was no doubt in David's mind, his Rachel was the most beautiful, most regal, most elegant woman in the world.

GWEN AND RACHEL stood with their chosen men before the minister who had watched Rachel grow from a babe-in-arms to a lovely young woman. Both couples pledged to love and honor each other until they were parted by death.

Gwen doubted that most young mortals who undertook this vow had anywhere near as clear an understanding of those words as did Rachel and David.

She doubted that she truly understood how long eternity could be, but she knew she wouldn't want to face it without Lorenzo by her side.

The audience applauded thunderously when the newly married couples were presented to them.

Mr. and Mrs. David Evan Milligan.

Mr. and Mrs. Lorenzo Alan Santini.

Two new unions were now complete

David whooped, and swung his new wife in a circle. "Let the party begin."

Renzo and Gwen beamed as the four friends fairly danced down the aisle. They raced through the passageway and to the deck below. Arriving at the area designated for the receiving line, Rachel and Gwen squealed and hugged each other in delight. Renzo and David radiated pride, enthusiastically shaking hands — each congratulating the other on winning the second best woman in the world.

The yacht was perfect for a celebration such as this. As the guests left the ceremony for the receiving line, young men quietly appeared to transform the room. While the guests enjoyed an elegant buffet on the deck below, the room was readied for its second incarnation. The dais where the minister and the bridal couples had stood now held a talented jazz band and the floor was cleared to make room for dancing. There was also the observation deck, where hardy souls could stroll and enjoy the winter wind in their hair as they watched the sights on the riverbank glide past.

What a perfect afternoon.

Renzo and Gwen cut their cake and fed each other delicate morsels, to the crowd's delight. Gwen was much too excited to sit demurely and eat, so the *Old One* couple circulated among the tables, greeting old friends and introducing themselves to Rachel's myriad relatives.

When the deck above was ready to receive revelers, the ship's steward made the announcement. David and Rachel, Renzo and

Gwen made their way to the dance floor for their first dance as married couples. On the second waltz, Rachel danced with her father, Gwen with Uncle Jem, David with his mother, and Renzo, because he had no close family in attendance, drew Katie onto the dance floor.

All in all it was a wonderful day. All of Elizabeth's careful—though hurried— planning went off without a flaw. As it neared time for the celebration to end, Gwen and Renzo made their way to the observation deck. Few of the guests had made the effort to stroll outside. For even though the winter sun was bright and clear on this glorious day, the air was chill. Add to that the wind created by the motion of the yacht, and most people were glad to do their celebrating in the warmth of the enclosed decks.

Glancing around to be certain they were alone, Renzo sketched a sigil to provide them with a buffer of warmth. They walked slowly, hand in hand, the length of the ship, stopping at last in the bow. Gwen snuggled into the safety of Renzo's arms as they stared down the river at their approaching mooring.

"So, Mr. Santini, where do we go from here?" Gwen's words were a quiet purr of contentment, but Renzo had no trouble hearing her above the hum of the engines. He was an *Old One*, and he was attuned to his wife.

"If you mean, the moment we dock, I have a honeymoon surprise for you." Renzo kissed the tip of her nose as Gwen raised delighted eyes to meet his own. "If you mean in the coming years... well, I doubt High Magic is going to let us sit idle." He traced the outline of the recently created medallion as he spoke.

"That's really what I was wondering." She nodded gripping the cool metal in her fist. Merlin had given her a beautifully wrought chain to support the medallion, which she now wore around her neck. "I mean, I finished my quest. The seven signs joined to create this medallion. There must be a purpose for it. I wonder what it is, and when I'll find out?"

"All in due time, my love. All in due time. For the moment, let's just enjoy a well-deserved rest." Renzo bent closer to her enticing lips. "When the time is right, High Magic will make our path clear." He kissed her.

As his lips touched hers— warm, secure and vibrantly alive— Gwen sent a tendril of thought curling into his mind.

And they lived happily ever after ...

Through all eternity.

Their lips parted in triumphant smiles, and then Renzo deepened his kiss, and Gwen forgot about the long future that lay open before them. She nestled securely into Renzo's warm embrace...

...into the wonderful gift of this glorious moment.

ALSO BY DEBBIE MUMFORD

Kristi Lundrigan Mysteries:

- DELECTABLE MOUNTAIN QUILTING (NOVEL)
- IN A PICKLE (NOVEL)
- FOOL'S PUZZLE (SHORT STORY)
- WILDFIRE! (SHORT STORY)

Gus and Ghost Short Story Series:

- SEVENTH
- SEVENTH: FIRST FRUITS
- DEATH OF AN ALCHEMIST (UNCOLLECTED ANTHOLOGY)
- SEVENTH: THE SAMHAIN DILEMMA
- DARK OF THE MOON (UNCOLLECTED ANTHOLOGY)

Logans of Lastalrig Series:

- HER HIGHLAND LAIRD (NOVELLA)
- HER HIGHLAND YULE (SHORT STORY)

Red's Series:

- RED'S MAGICK (SHORT STORY COLLECTION)
- SEEING RED (SHORT STORY)

Signs of the Prophecy Novels:

- YOUNGEST
- SEEKER

- CHOSEN (COMING SOON!)

Witchling Short Story Series:

- WITCHLING
- THE SOLITARY SORCERESS
- TO PROTECT A PRINCESS

Stand Alone Novels:

- SECOND SIGHT

Historical Fiction:

- HER HIGHLAND LAIRD (NOVELLA)
- HER HIGHLAND YULE
- INCIDENT ON THE HIGH LINE
- MISS BAINBRIDGE'S SUMMER ADVENTURE
- MISS BAINBRIDGE'S CHRISTMAS PARTY
- SISTERS IN SUFFRAGE
- THE TRAIL WHERE WE CRIED
- THE WHITE DRAGON AND THE RED

Short Story Collections:

- LOVE IN A FLASH
- TALES OF BYGONE DAYS
- TALES OF LOVE & MAGICK
- TALES OF THE UNEXPECTED
- TALES OF TOMORROW
- TALES OF DISASTROUS DEEDS

Short Fiction:

- A GROVE OF MOUNTAIN ASH
- A WALK WITH GEORGIA

- Astromancer
- Because of the Christmas Stroll
- Beneath and Beyond
- Deep Dreaming
- Delia's Decision
- Egg Thief
- Ice Storm
- Incident on the High Line
- In Search of a Valentinian
- Miss Bainbridge's Christmas Party
- Miss Bainbridge's Summer Adventure
- Needle-Green
- New Year
- Opening Her Eyes
- Remembrance
- Silver-Tipped Death
- Simon Says
- Sisters in Suffrage
- Skye Dreams
- Spinning
- The Tie That Binds
- The Trail Where We Cried
- The White Dragon and the Red
- To Dream of Flying
- Treasures
- Trial on the Trail
- Wakinyan's Valley

"WDM Presents" Anthologies:

- Tales of Mystery & Mayhem
- 2016: A Year of Short Fiction
- 2017: A Year of Short Fiction
- WDM Presents: Short Fiction from 2018

If you enjoyed *Seeker*, you may want to read *Her Highland Laird*, a time-travel novella set in the Highlands of Scotland. Here's a sample chapter.

Cat Logan wandered through Edinburgh in a dreamy glow. The musical lilt of the inhabitants' speech delighted her almost as much as the easy juxtaposition of ancient and contemporary architecture. Everywhere she turned, she discovered new reference points for her recently acquired degree in medieval literature, as well as her clan heritage. The Logans of Lasterrick had left an indelible mark on Edinburgh.

Each day brought new revelations, and she blessed Gran Da for his extravagant graduation gift. Life had been hard for both of them since her father's death, but Gran Da had been determined to celebrate Cat's achievement in style.

"I'm so proud of you, Cat," he had said, draping an arm around her shoulders. "I only wish your mother and father could be here to share this day."

"Me, too, Gran Da." Cat nestled into her grandfather's embrace and blessed the fates who had given her into this dear old man's care. Gran Da had welcomed her father and his infant daughter home after Cat's mother had died. Complications from Cat's entrance into the world had robbed her father of his wife and Cat of her mother, but she'd never felt any stigma of blame. Gran Da had been there for them. He had provided warmth and stability in Cat's life while her father had pursued his military career.

But David Logan, a high-ranking air force pilot, had died in a training accident last year. Cat and Gran Da had both been devastated by his loss.

As if to punctuate Cat's need for a European vacation, her ex-fiancé Brent Myers had chosen the night before graduation to announce he'd fallen out of love with Cat and into bed with Ariana Davidson.

She'd given that scumball four years of her life. Why had he asked her to marry him if he hadn't been certain she was the woman he wanted to spend his life with? Why had she accepted? How could she have missed a character flaw that allowed such blatant disloyalty and unfaithfulness? Obviously, her judgment sucked when it came to good-looking men.

Gran Da had taken the defection in stride.

"I'm sorry, love," he said quietly when Cat informed him of the broken engagement. "I won't discuss it further, if that's yer wish, but ye need tae ken I'm nae surprised. I've a bit o' the sight, an' I've always known ye were destined for an unexpected path. Nothin' about Brent was unexpected.

"Go tae Scotland, darlin' girl, an' if opportunity arises, ne'er look back. I've a feelin' in me bones ... Scotland holds yer future."

~

On her third day in Edinburgh, a previously undiscovered lane beckoned. She hesitated. If the most ancient byways were also the narrowest, allowing the least penetration of the summer sun, this one qualified as the oldest of the old. The narrow passage drew her, the near-compulsion reminding her of Gran Da's remarks about second sight. Curiosity won out over caution, and she followed her instincts to a shabby, little establishment near the midpoint of the narrow lane.

Cat studied the grimy window of the ancient thrift shop. The interior appeared as black as the tarnished silver door knocker. Did she really want to push past the door and breach the musty interior? She'd passed a reputable-looking antique shop two blocks back; perhaps she should browse there.

Yet, the same indescribable *something* that had pulled her past the clean, well- kept shop and into this narrow lane prompted her to linger.

Follow your heart, her grandsire's voice whispered in her mind. But why would her heart lead her to a second-hand junk shop in a forgotten district of Edinburgh?

She'd never learn the answer if she was too cowardly to cross the threshold. Expelling a sigh, she straightened her shoulders, grasped the doorknob, and turned.

An old-fashioned bell tinkled, and she stepped into the little store. A single bulb dangled from the ceiling, barely lighting the dark recesses of the room. Shelves towered against the walls, and stacks of shabby furniture obscured the floor. Cat wended a careful path between tottering stacks of rubbish.

She lingered over a yellowing baptismal gown for an infant, fingering the fine lace and admiring the tiny, precise stitches of the hand-sewn seams. Hard to imagine that all clothing had once been sewn by dedicated women. And men. Mustn't forget the tailors of the world.

"May I help ye fin' somethin', miss?"

Cat gasped and dropped the gown. She hadn't noticed anyone in the gloom of the shop. An elderly man with stringy, grey hair and stubbly jaw stood behind a sturdy wood counter — the only flat surface in the shop not covered with a jumble of knick- knacks.

"No thank you," she said with a little smile. "I'm just looking."

"Nae many Americans stop to browse in my wee shop."

"My accent gave me away?"

"Aye, lassie. Nae a body will mistake ye for a Scot."

She sighed and turned back to the baptismal gown. "That's too bad because my roots are here."

"Ahh," he breathed. "Sae you're one o' those. Searchin' for yer ancestry, are ye? What's yer surname?"

"Logan. I've traced my family back to Sir Robert of Lasterrick."

"Well, then," he said, smug satisfaction lighting his homely face, "Ye've come tae th' right shop. I happen tae hae a relic of Sir Robert's only son, Sir Eideard Logan. We'd name him Edward today."

He rounded the counter and scuttled between rows of merchandise to a tall shelf at the back. Opening a ladder, he climbed to the top with surprising agility and poked his hand behind a grimy vase. Carefully, he withdrew his prize and returned to the floor of the shop.

Cat sidled over to join him, her heart beating a quick tattoo against her chest. "What is it?" she asked, breathless with anticipation.

"A silver casket," he replied, revealing a tarnished silver box roughly the size of a ream of paper.

Cat stretched out her hand to stroke the embossed lid.

"'Tis rumored tae contain Sir Eddie's heart."

"Eww!" She snatched her hand back and buried it in her pocket.

The shopkeeper laughed, a full, rich sound that bounced off the ceiling and skittered among the piles of rubble.

She smiled wanly. "Don't you know what's in the box?"

"Nay, miss. 'Twould take a braver man than me tae open this box. 'Tis cursed, ye

see."

Now it was Cat's turn to laugh. "Cursed? You believe in such nonsense?"

The man nodded gravely. "Aye, lassie, I dae, an' sae should ye if ye ken what's good for ye." He turned back to the ladder and started to climb.

Cat's heart leapt. Her instincts screamed that the silver casket held a secret — that its contents had drawn her to this dusty little shop.

"Wait," she cried. "Please."

The man paused. He studied her face with narrowed eyes, glanced at the casket, and then nodded. Stepping back to the ground, he led the way to his counter and gently placed the casket upon it.

Cat followed him, and this time her hands ignored her brain. They cradled the tarnished box, stroking the ornamented surface of the lid.

"Here now, miss. Ye're gettin' filthy. Let me clean 'at up."

Gently, he disengaged the casket from her reluctant fingers and wiped it with a soft cloth. The more he rubbed, the more Cat itched to hold the casket again. Finally, when she could bear the separation no longer, she pulled the box back and stared at the now gleaming lid.

"Are those words?"

The shopkeeper adjusted his glasses and cocked his head. "Aye. There's an inscription."

"Can you read it?"

"Probably. But nae if ye clutch it sae."

A nervous giggle escaped her lips. "I'm sorry. I don't know what's gotten into me." She shoved the casket across the counter to him.

He turned the lid to the light and read in a halting voice, "Catriona, return to me my heart. Lastalrig Castle. By the bright of the moon. Eideard."

Apprehension seized Cat's throat and squeezed. Her vision swam, and her fingers tingled. She clung to consciousness by sheer force of will.

"What ...." Her voice croaked and died. She moistened her dry lips, cleared her throat, and spoke again. "What was that name?"

He stared at her with open curiosity. "Catriona. It's th' auld form of Katherine."

"I know. My name is Catriona Logan."

Look for *Her Highland Laird* at your favorite online retailer.

ABOUT DEBBIE MUMFORD

Debbie Mumford specializes in speculative fiction—fantasy, paranormal romance, and science fiction. Author of the popular *Sorcha's Children* series, Debbie loves the unknown, whether it's the lure of space or earthbound mythology. Her work has been published in multiple volumes of *Fiction River*, as well as in *Heart's Kiss Magazine*, *Spinetingler Magazine*, and other popular markets. She writes about dragon-shifters, time-traveling lovers, and ghostly detectives for adults as Debbie Mumford and contemporary fantasy for tweens and young adults as Deb Logan.

Join Debbie's special announcement newsletter list and receive a FREE story!

To learn more, visit Debbie at:
debbiemumford.com/
Or send her an email at:
deborah.mumford@gmail.com

f facebook.com/DebbieMumfordWrites
a amazon.com/author/debbiemumford
BB bookbub.com/authors/debbie-mumford
twitter.com/deborah_mumford